wrong bar

wrong bar

nathaniel g. moore

Tightrope Books

Tightrope Books
602 Markam Street
Toronto, Ontario
Canada M6G 2L8
www.tightropebooks.com

Canada Council for the Arts   Conseil des Arts du Canada

ONTARIO ARTS COUNCIL
CONSEIL DES ARTS DE L'ONTARIO

EDITOR: Shirarose Wilensky
COVER DESIGN: Karen Correia Da Silva
COVER PHOTO: Geoffrey Pugen
ILLUSTRATIONS: Amanda Sampson
TYPESETTING: Shirarose Wilensky

Produced with the support of the Canada Council for the Arts and the Ontario Arts Council.

PRINTED IN CANADA.

LIBRARY AND ARCHIVES CANADA CATALOGUING IN PUBLICATION

Moore, Nathaniel G., 1974–

Wrong bar / Nathaniel G. Moore.

ISBN 978-1-926639-02-4

I. Title.

PS8626.O595W76 2009   C813'.6   C2009-903912-5

go fish

I groped in my pockets, fished out what I needed, and shot him dead, as he lunged at me; then he fell on his face, as if sunstruck on the parade ground, at the feet of his king. None of the serried tree trunks looked his way, and I fled, still clutching Dagmara's lovely little revolver.

—Vladimir Nabokov, *Look at the Harlequins!*

part one
kill the headlights and put it in neutral

1.

This dingy morning is half eaten.

The store feels empty.

I have been fidgeting by the colourful fish tanks with their hyper-turquoise glamour burbling in the reflection, while outside a prehistoric wind terrifies me with its malignant hissing; it wreathes harsh against the glass with the finesse of a poltergeist. Well, not finesse. It's smearing the glass in a certain inhumane way: entirely relentless. Maybe finesse, maybe calculating.

A customer prods me with sea queries, reminding me I am not alone. The store is not empty.

"So they last a long time?" The woman is rushed; her eyes go across the tanks, over to a hamster wheel, and back to me. To me, she seems erratic and disenfranchised, not fully comprehending her role as caregiver.

"You'd be surprised," I go. "How many would you like?" Then, giving a half-crescent smile, "As you *may* know, it's half-price fish day here at Sloppy Salmon's Wet Pet Centre."

I add the word "wet" for syllabic resonance. Ten in the morning, four customers, and my face is already a clock of sweat, my skin iridescent and convivial. That's probably not the right word. My skin tingles in chatter, if tingles could speak. Not tingles so much as itches.

Maybe it's glue or something.

The mother asks her son what he thinks. The kid shrugs. I begin to unravel, not literally, of course—"Look, I'm under cover," I tell them. I feel light-headed. "This is a sting operation."

The kid has a blinding blue windbreaker on.

So the mother stops petting her son's head and looks up like I've been in a coffin the whole time and she's been looking down on me and suddenly I've opened my eyes and started singing "Fools Rush In." It's exactly that sort of look that she is wearing, and she opens her mouth in slow motion, "Excuse me?"—with an extra long vowel at the end (she's holding onto the E, lower facial muscles in a MMMMM-EEE-EEE-EEE-EEE-EEE-EEE-EEE-EEE-EEE-EEE pose long after she drops the last percussive syllable). Her teeth are bright and she looks as if she has just hit Pause. I want to fill in her gums and smear her teeth with the fish food flakes just for fun. It would look like scabs dissolving. IT WOULD.

The fish are nibbling on crusty matter; their tank is as loud as pigeons, and they're becoming unmitigated live-stock right before my eyes.

"The fish you are buying are part of my operative. These Albino Butterflies are also, well, singularly, let's say the Albino Butterfly was-slash-is the title of an unpublished piece of short fiction based on a Londordia College residency sorta sofa-like fling I had in 1995 and has been suffocating my life for over a decade."

"Excuse me?" The woman is rummaging through her purse. When she stops, I assume it's because she's found the mace.

"If you *really* want the story I can mail it to you. I don't have *any* extra copies with me."

The woman appears perplexed, a strange out-of-focus concern pours over her face. Maudlin is that sort of city: always sort of off. I can hear the store's phone begin to ring ever so gently, my liver being pecked at in percussive, strange-splitting tears and pulls. Each ring, another liver bite.

"Do you need food with them?" I ask. "Hold on, I have a call. I can hear the phone." I turn around. "I'll be right back. Keep your eyes on the fish, don't trust them . . . So, food, yes? For the fish?"

The woman nods.

"I'll get you two months worth. That way you don't

5

have to come back so often."

"Sounds good to me. And we want *seven* fish."

"Seven." The small child says. "I want seven." He is about eight.

I understand the future. As I'm walking away I can feel their aqua eyes on me; fish have grammatical pupils. When I pick up the phone I notice the kid pointing at the tank aggressively; although I can't tell for sure, it's possible he's even making contact with the glass, a serious violation of store policy.

"Look kid, don't haul anchor on these young pups now, they need *lots* of love." He looks at me strange-faced, so I go, "I think."

The phone: "Sloppy Salmon's, can I help thee?"

It's Cate. She's telling me things that are disturbing. Cate's my intern; more on her later—she's calling back in five.

"Okay," I tell Cate. I hang up the phone. I roll up my sleeves and walk back to the kid and mother.

I keep my eye on a red door directly at the back. I do this for good reason: behind the door is a small storage room where three employees have been quarantined, so to speak; their name tags glowing rich and rosy under a variety of light sources—different lights for different species—all red and green and yellow back there. I am worried they'll lose hair when I remove their duct-tape gags, duct-tape handcuffs, and duct-tape ankle fetters. By reading their body language with my acute empathy and ability to prognosticate, I can ascertain their various levels of hunger. I will try to sound casual but genuine. I will describe the food I have ordered for them—in theory.

Back to my job. The kid's nose is pressed against the tank; it looks like he's an oinker, a prize-winning ham on a day pass, staring at fish under glass.

"I like those guys, Mom," I hear the kid go.

"Excellent," I say, looking to the woman for approval. I begin my "act natural" routine with the fish. I have a little net, and two fish are flipping around in it. "Seven, okay . . . ready?"

The woman nods, fondling her BlackBerry. The fish are stupid. The kid is so happy.

Dipping the little green net into the tank, I capture two more, then three, until I've loaded the seven fish into the plastic bag full of water. Some are clearly leapers—not lepers, *leapers*—a few inches into the air they go with demonstrative anger, right off the net's micro grill. I carry them to the cash register. The kid stares into the plastic bag. The Albino Butterflies pantomime modest agitation, swatting one another with their yellow fins. It's a bit dramatic.

The kid goes, "Why are vey doing dat?" in his sloppy kid voice, which I find forced and degrading. He's probably home-schooled.

"Those fish are very emotional. Better not piss them off. They'll hold a *real* evil grudge."

I return the credit card to the mother.

Again with the phone. I turn my back to the sale, a real no-no. "Settle? Settle for what? An anonymous call? A phony claim? Never! It's not just their money that's at stake, it's our integrity. You damn well ride these evildoers to Hell's larynx, okay Cate?"

The mother wrenches the pale kid and the fish out the door. The store vibrates in electronic adjustments and physical acumen: buzzing, chiming, red-eyed synapses a-blazing, the rudimentary electronic eye bats, calculating proximity and girth. The store is now empty. I can hear the faint struggle in the back room and turn up the radio.

"Charles, you there? Pick up," Cate goes. I've put the receiver down on the counter.

"Hello, Cate?" I can detect her pain. Even though I can't see her, Cate is visibly upset, disgusted for believing that justice exists. "In this world, Cate, nothing is certain."

I listen to her talk about her day. Her investigation has proven once and for all exactly what I alone once suspected: the existence of an illegal domestic fish farm crime ring—"Right here in Maudlin City! Harsh growth conditions, Charles, real harsh. Steroids in the eyes, fucked up water sources, and really, really shoddy fish feeders. The breeding tanks haven't been properly cleaned and would

8

never pass inspection."

"It's Bethlehem all over again. We have to move in," I say, checking the store's surveillance monitors. "We have no choice now. It's pure war."

"But they'll just dump the poor little guys, thousands of them, if we, you know, call the police."

I feel for her. And for the fish.

"Cate, if we let these guppy fraud bastards ride rough-shod over the laws of this land, it will be utter chaos for eternity. It's not me; you see, I'm fine with it, but the lit-tle kids out there who have to take these phony guppies home—then what happens? They have a sleepover one night and their friends are like, those guppies you have are so fake, Jimmy. Then you know what happens? They turn to crime . . . whoring, drugging, organized sports, poetry."

"Okay. What time do you have?" Cate asks.

"Not sure. I'm done here just before six. Say, Cate . . ."

"Yeah?"

"You wear a belt or suspenders?" I migrate vertically behind the cash register. South.

"Suspenders. Why?"

I imagine Cate shifting her weight to one side as she tries to crop her surveillance photography on her phone *and* put on lip gloss. Her lips are full; she wears this really pale makeup so her stark green eyes come at you from this phantom-like tableau of skin. It's mesmerizing, but she's so sarcastic. But she's helpful. The truth is, I don't know what I'd do without her. I'd certainly never solve all the mysteries surrounding my misfortunes in publishing, let alone solve Maudlin City's phony, nay, diluted, fish fraud crisis.

"Suspenders, you say? Hmm. That's good. This cover of mine is nuts. A pet store! Like I know the first thing about fish. I'm a poet, for Christ's sake. I'm Maudlin City freelance!"

More and more I think of the employees all tied up and how hungry they must be. How they might have started eating less fish since starting work at Sloppy's.

Before ambushing the employees, I had taken a two-day trip three towns over. I was just rummaging around, trying to get my head around some key issues of my identity, when I found myself in a crappy hamburger joint. I am pretty savvy when it comes to current events, and when I heard something about a rotten fish farming operation and these guys in a booth behind me going, "KEEP YOUR VOICE DOWN, LENNY" and "WE'RE EXPANDING TO MAUDLIN CITY, SEE . . . " and talking about how they needed an established storefront to sell their weak fish, well, I went all gumshoe and began jotting things down. Life is all about being at odd places and . . . thinking.

For two days I trolled like a shadow through Leatherpalm, dodging spoon reflections, tampering with another city, dipping my own perverse magnet into the ground. I shadowed like dry cleaning. Like felt-tipped pens on the shelf.

After a few eerie eavesdropping sessions it was clear: everything would lead to Sloppy's. That was the store they picked.

"Then it's settled," they went. These really gamey, dock-type men. They were peeing. Coughing . . .

"Sloppy's in Maudlin. We'll dump the first batch there, just a delivery, bait and switch."

"Nice one, Frank!"

So I run into these guys again two nights later, this time at the laundromat. Again with their weak, crazy, strung-out-on-mercury-water-fish-hatchery plots.

The store smells like a gerbil wheel.

"We're hot on something. Stay close to the phone and draw the blinds," I tell Cate.

"I'm outside," Cate goes.

Now, apron on, employees safe and gagged, I have it all, everything required for putting them away, these small-town fish meanies. Read outs, water samples, distribution invoices, and tons of photos. Cate is right, though: the fish'll die if I call this in, even an anonymous tip. And, somehow, the Maudlin literary scene is also in on it. There's no way that sixteen of the city's twenty literary magazines are, just by coincidence, having sea-themed escape issues.

It's like they're begging to get caught.

Must have dozed off. The cash register screen reads 3:35 p.m. A few more minutes before I can untie the employees and meet Cate. To distract myself from pangs of guilt and excess anxiety due to all the malicious work prevention I've doctored in the back room, I unfold a short story and begin to calmly read it.

Cate has noted this particular copy to death. My eyes have grazed this story a thousand times. Cate's little scrawls are all over the margins; after passages that begin and end with time references, for example, and overstated instances of "homemade lime curtains," Cate would write in brackets sometimes: [How can you prove that? The time. Why is your stuff so time-specific? You have some sort of time-coded bad-vibe memory-archival thing, like a burned tattoo time code in your department of sad state of affairs]. I'll explain:

> A Monday afternoon on the porous lawn outside of Hingston Hall. It's the beginning. Dagmara. [Porous lawn? Come on. Wet lawn, moist, damp, but porous?] It's the ending. Dagmara, a fairy with tiny fangs.

It's thirteen years later and the story is still an edifice

scaffolding, a smudged relic without sensation. It's definitely the ending. It's overdraft and without end. The story opens slowly and goes downhill from there: Dagmara was sitting on the lawn. The partially wet grass. I was thin and pale and ready to reveal my inner gloom. In the 1990s this was called foreplay. The editors of magazines were like, it's well written but there seems to be no relationship between the narrator and Dagmara. And that's *my* fault? I guess it is.

The phone rings. Cate is chirpy, "Okay, so the grass is tall and *she's* like a giraffe?" She's following the instructions I laid out for her perfectly. Some calls will be about writing, some about slum fish crime rings. Just in case someone is listening—which they are.

"It's Fiction Editing Tuesday here at the Charles Haas Centre for the Arts."

And it's all part of the cover: to throw off any possible coverts. Just another routine author-intern phone meeting. No surveillance or fish ring detective work going on here.

"I'm reading from this blue draft here," Cate goes, "but maybe we should quit the editing for a bit and concentrate on this, you know, fish piracy story.

"Right. *That* story."

She's eating an apple or bones or something. I look outside; the sky is bright and gaping. I fold the pages of fiction back up into their repetitive creases. Cate just sent images from her cell to the computer here at the store. I picture her inside a large cardboard box with a tinfoil helmet.

"You get the images?" Cate asks. Her voice crackles like a forest fire, yet I don't fear for her safety. She is convincingly calm.

"We can't go in front of a jury with this!" I tell her.

"We're not in front of a jury yet!" Cate is on the ball. Uncovering this fishy crime ring is the best way ever to start a work week. I feel so inspired sometimes.

Cate is suggesting new operative names: "Operation Tilapia?"

"No!" I go. "Forget it. This is Operation Gemini. Forget Albino Butterfly. That mother and son duo didn't fool me one bit, they are totally associate editors—one of them is. I swear I've seen them at a reading somewhere. Every sea-themed issue is just a front! This is bigger than I thought. They must be using the money they save from the inadequate fish exchange to pay for their magazine printing. We should crunch the numbers again later this week. That mom and kid are already on the horn to every literary magazine in this country. Cate, you put every magazine under surveillance!"

"I was about to suggest that."

"They can't keep up this act. This evil ring of cruel fish farming in North America must end. This will not become another terrible trend. I will not tolerate guppy and gold-fish mutation, not on my watch!"

"They're bound to crack. So, standard operation?"

"What's that involve again?" I go, catching a reflection of myself in a mirror. I'm cocking an eyebrow now. "They're all in on it, Cate, and now they know you know. And they know you know me."

"Standard ops are: microphone, tape recorder, 3 mm camera, daytime coverage . . . fake interns. The works."

"And at nighttime the fish gangsters can go out schmoozing to Maudlin lit functions? Forget it! We have to do better than that."

"A microphone in every room, telescopic lens, mail bugs . . . Whatever you want, Charles."

"Maybe. They can't keep up with our marvellous edits and blood-hound tracking senses, but *we* can keep up with their evil plans."

Cate goes, "Let's stick with the plan."

I start to cough, tears rush from my eyes like danger. I am completely muddled.

"Truth be told, Cate, I'm a sick carp on its last shallow lake stride."

"Maybe you should get out of there soon."

"Hold on Cate, meet me at you-know-where in about two hours. I gotta take this call."

"Okay."

I duck down to tie my shoelaces.

"Oh, hello, Mr O'Brien. That's all right. Yes, we have that on order. Two packages of the Tropical Refresher. Yes, it's a fine product. I'll call you when it's in. Yes, taking the lunches at the store, you know I'm a busy man. Can you just hold? Thanks." CLICK.

"Cate, you there?"

"Charles, I'm at that half pipe tunnel you and Dagmara went under before the Blur concert. Those magazine editors are not here. Should I check this location off the list?" Cate asks, playing along with our decoy operative script verbatim.

"For now. We'll go back in a few days. Next stop, The Spectrum on St. Catherine's Street."

"Sure thing." CLICK.

"Mr O'Brien, sorry about that, now listen, you want the two bags of the Tropical Refresher, right? CLICK.

"Hello, Cate?" Nothing. CLICK.

"Sorry Mr O'Brien, you were saying? Certainly. I understand." CLICK.

"Okay employees in the back. Who's hungry? I'll be releasing you now. Remember that Mr O'Brien is a bit confused so you'll have some backpeddling to do with him in the days to come. You see, I had a slightly different figure in mind. And he claims to have no idea what I'm talking about, but most of the time these magazine editors speak in riddles. Now I know what you're going to say when I remove these gags—that I am being grotesque. Well let me tell you something, as one member of the working elite to another, if this city wants a knockdown fight, Cate and I'll give it to them. And no compromise!"

I slip out of my cursed pet store apron and return to my suit and tie. I leave a note for the pizza delivery person to untie the employees. It's not a very clever note, just sorta simple, with an arrow pointing the way.

I meet Cate in the mall. Her hair looks awesome. It's cut short and dyed fire-engine red. She has a small television set under her left arm, barely noticeable.

"So you talk to this Dagmara ever, from the story?"

"No. We try, but it's always strange. She called a moth an Albino Butterfly; I had written a poem about a moth you see—"

"Right," Cate goes.

"There was a Nabokov quote about Dagmara and a gun," I tell her. "A lovely little revolver."

"And by quote you mean made up by you?"

"No, it's real. Dagmara didn't buy it."

"Right. I sent all the fish documents to your home by courier. And a copy to City Hall."

"Good. We'll figure all this out by Monday."

"Here good?" Cate asks, pointing to a sushi hut in the food court.

"Yes, I'm starving."

Tea concealed in plastic, rivers of soy and wasabi, bits of sesame on the rice—I love it when they do that. The spicy tuna is perfect, and I even like the miso soup. Cate finishes her sushi first.

"Let's walk through the mall to the bus stop," she says.

Cate leads me along the first aisle of a department store (towels and pajamas), occasionally extending her wooly arms all aviator-like. I follow suit in my human helicopter.

"What the hell are you doing?" Cate asks, noticing my spins and erratic sound effects.

"Didn't really think this one out," I confess.

We are swelled winter coats and suffocating and simulated fevers.

"We should go that way," Cate says, pointing to the exit. "I have to be at the airport by six, and it's looking kind of gloomy. Supposed to snow something awful."

As Cate lures me outdoors, I am hit by a dust crop of fragrance; the sinister counters are always positioned by the exits, as if to hint the city into smelling, offering agitation to the pedestrian senses, enticing all with trendy hints of elite vapours.

"I want to check out the hardware for a moment, Cate."

I eschew an awkward couple on the escalator because

I want to be delighted at the display of outdoor hardware I know awaits me: a row of glistening snow blowers, each one red, diligent, and silent, awaiting a task, curated to destroy. I look deep into a machine's open cache: the finer points of its digestive tract, its teeth gritty rows of talcumed steel in faint oil cologne intrigue me more than if doctors were showing me high definition footage of my tasking brain, governing all this convexity.

"Cate, if only my stomach were as complex, if only man could be stainless steel and real blade grit with such symmetry and intent."

"Yeah, if only," Cate says. "You look pale," she continues, her hand on my forehead. "You feel okay?"

I am now on my knees before the glistening red blowers.

"If only my teeth were as industrial, Cate. Dear, oh dear."

Cate shakes her head. "Things work out at the store? I mean, did you untie everyone?"

"Of course. Ordered them a pizza." I feel woozy and clutch a boxed microwave.

"Seriously Charles, you look pale."

"It must be the hemoglobin lighting: sick housefly brown, these fluorescent bulbs from Denmark root-canal me every time. Spiritually. Maybe I need a thumbtack . . . a mint . . . a nap or a magnetic bath."

Cate remains silent. I can hear her breathing, and it's more than soothing. The security cameras sway their necks to and fro.

"Don't worry, Cate, we'll get outside, we'll go our separate ways."

"I'm sure of that," she says. "I'll see you next week though?"

I leaf through my wallet: an invoice, cedar chips for rodents, organic kelp orders, a note that reads "goat cheese."

Where laughter could have risen out on a grid, on its own separate track (lever pushed up, entering the audio's thick multi-leveled nuance), a truck belches, a bus exhales, and winter's malicious choir belts out its finest renditions. I look at the malnourished trees cinched together in sparse soil, potted and thumbed in a shallow grave in the parking lot. Barely six people in the parking lot: a gamey man and his buddies, a lone security guard, a gaggle of teen wolves slowly evaporating into the grey nightline horizon framed by rotten television wires.

I sing the most beautiful hymn on earth: "Dried pineapple faces, sunken, hollow, and sore, how you hallmark a healthy regimen in me . . . You are the thunderclap, the seven-hour nightmare, you're how I'll survive in a pupa, the pupa I'll be fetal within . . . and, oh, how my wings will soar me and, oh, how my kingdom will ignore me, pupa pupa, do not forget me . . . take me on your special ingestion quest."

Across the street Cate is checking the bus schedule. She's waving me over, ducking into the gas station store. I am under a large tree.

"Give me paradise," I go.

These are the typical exercises Cate puts me through for my writing, tearing apart the city brick by brick to solve mysterious inconsistencies, from the smallest guppy with a lump on its side to an out-of-place veranda brick. We really get into it, like horseplay in a pool.

Crossing the street I watch the Don Mills 25 bus go south; knowing that Cate is destined to be consumed by this bus and its route shortly. Cate is in line, sifting through soda straws with her hands in fingerless gloves.

"You want anything? A drink?" she goes.

I am recalling, with much arousal, a pupa poetry book from a few years ago. A big hit in Maudlin's contemporary history, it was really quite critically acclaimed. I am staring up at the branch of this tree, fantasizing about my larval state. I am a firm believer that while the old short story or poem is being digested, the new version is excreted. I close my eyes and for a moment fall asleep, just as the last car exits the lot, two small red circles narrowing to tiny artificial specks in the vast uncomplicated night.

The undulating night of faint stars is now netted over me, tacking my phony wings completely still. I am now standing behind Cate, who is next in line. She turns toward me. She looks at her watch, the cash register, with all the prowling quality of a sad shoplifter. Cate's face looks weepy and cold. I am obsessed with my inability to scare potential predators, write poetry, and even digest the mint I believe I am chewing. In the pupa, if I had one, I would wear pleated pants and condense my mass by doubling up my arms and legs into a neat fold, as a translucent layer crawls along my back. With its mind, the tree is now holding me tightly. Parking lot trees have collaborative toxins that would make me unpalatable to birds and other predators. My layers are now realized; I have come this far, colourless and deranged. The city is dulling into dark grey soup.

"I have to get to the airport to meet Daniel."

"Why? I haven't heard you speak of him in some time."

"Daniel is travelling tonight on a plane," Cate goes.

2.

Pen*tap"o*dy, n.
A measure or series consisting of five feet.

Early July is always a loud affair: nights pulled apart by laughter and devout urban rituals, burning schoolhouses, screamers, the pyrotechnic picnic that clobbers the big, gaping sky in random heat sprays of colliding phantoms. The screams match the climax, almost as though the voices are dubbing the action in psychedelic animation. I just downed 12 mg of Soderiaz, a stabilizing drug my doctor suggests will rob me of my paranoid feelings of mummification.

I pull into my dry dog of a driveway in my dead dog of a car. No matter how many times I pluck the sinewy weeds from the cracks here, they return all fresh and stoic. That's what I surmise, pulling my medium-sized frame on corduroy legs from the car to the house, feeling out of breath, parts of me rimmed in dirty sand.

That beach just after midnight though, what a solace; it always calms me some. I mean, don't I seem much calmer from, like, just a while ago with Cate and the cocoon imagery and the suffocation fetish and all that? That's what this drug I'm on does, in between its synapse cattle prodding: it allows me to live and feast in little rivets of expression and human empathy—perhaps not my own, but anyway . . .

I go straight to bed. Tomorrow will be devoted to writing, and nothing in Maudlin City can stop me—lawsuits, restraining orders. I'm not supposed to talk like that anymore. Soderiaz, however, doesn't dictate my dialogue boxes or cerebral viaducts. *That's right, Charles*, I don't, but could, hear, if I took enough of the blue-and-copper-coloured pills.

I trail off to sleep; my mind is unkempt and over-drafted. Summer is half-chewed. Everything is half-something. I have just witnessed my twenty-ninth Canada Day.

I cannot sleep: maybe a story about a woman who has her tubes tied and then falls in love with her doctor performing the surgery; or a barista who is obsessed with her customer's shoes and socks, so distracted and obsessed with gazing at each extremity, she often scalds herself; or bitchy heiresses who talk diamonds and gold, real slumming hybrid clean cockteasers who surround themselves with the super-ugly, the super-dull, in a perverse vanity relocation program—a visible bait and switch; or a house of girls who never wash and talk dirty and have dirty bedrooms. Too literal—too Maudlin City open mic night. Or a man who misses his wife who's in another country, and as he's rushing to the airport with heartfelt passion, he accidentally leaves the front door open and one of his roommates, minutes later, is attacked when a burglar surprises him. Tentacles for feet. The police don't know the truth, but the reader may.

I turn on the computer and hit the white rectangle indicating another melee with myself and hand-to-eye coordination. This one I christen "They Suffocate At Night." It's all about my concern for Cate and her meet-up with Daniel, of whom she's spoken so little. The things I recall are as follows: they dine on seafood twice a month; he is homesick, an incredible singer, possibly married, and enjoys classical music. In the story there is a teary goodbye over calamari and a possible double-murder that happens moments after Daniel leaves his apartment to go to the airport to meet up with Cate. Daniel has a secret he cannot tell even Cate, and it's revealed at the end that his true nature is quite nautical. Of course, Cate won't really confess to me anything particularly accurate about her relationship with Daniel, so I have to make it up. The end of the story has Daniel with his wife in Spain, submerged in the late-night ocean, growing tentacles and making love underwater. Something like this:

> "I love you," Daniel said softly, his distorted reflection pixelated as their limbs submerged. Both sets of tentacles treaded and swam in the water. Their smooth Spanish mouths filled with water. "I always will." This must be underwater love, Daniel thought. And it truly was.

3.

As I wake I want the beach, the waves in particular. They have always impressed me. A permanent sonic welt at first menaces, and then soothes me. Each one is unique in its approach, and I don't know exactly when I began to notice their percussion, but there is probably a single moment, a single moment that astonished and plagued me. Majestic-sounding, the waves are inaudible from far away, though, and therefore a close-up privilege. So I like the waves and how unpretentious they are, how they operate in time-re-leased spheres, musical notes for an ongoing performance that controls and nudges the planet into infinite equa-tions, checks and balances; moves history, makes it, and plans the future. The waves are at once the most compli-cated and simplest entities in my world, a phantom blood that courses omnisciently. Upon returning home, I rarely scrub the scent of beach from my moody body, instead I lie on my back lawn until sunset.

I recall one thorough editing session a few months ago. I had just seen my twenty-ninth Easter Monday come and go. I remember clearly wearing light corduroy all day with much comfort and dignity, while fondly going over Cate's thoughtful notes on my fiction. Her quirky suggestions did more than traffic my stream-of-consciousness tendencies with the care of a child damming sandcastle moats with a clump of gentle logic, or wet sand, literally: "I want to put wet sand here, a big clump of it." Some of the sentences reminded her of a foul meal being served, a torrid pasta resembling reversed organs, fuming incoherently in pain. One scene sent her into facsimiles of a delinquent forest creature, taking a series of branches and prematurely snapping them from a budding maple or spruce. The phrase "terrible ending" also came up in her manicuring.

At 9:45 Cate lets herself in and makes some cat noises and brings out a plate of biscuits and steaming mugs of tea. She sits across from me.

"Need me to read anything, birthday man?"

I grunt something, running my hand across a series of pages, bookmarked magazines, and a bounty of strange scrawls.

"Some deadlines are coming up, right? Maybe we can work on those today."

Cate, like no other man or woman before her, has deployed an efficiency missile into the war zone of my dysfunctions—the parameters of which, she could tell from exhaustive inspection, are infinite. That is her gift. I watched her through the curtain moments earlier, sitting on my front porch, munching mango quarters softly, and I wished that somehow I would find a way to survive on the island of my own delicious mango pain.

"Cate, do you know about these wood wasps? The science guys think they are perfect for brain surgery. No joke."

"What?"

"They want to get robot wasps to mimic the patterns of wood wasps for brain tunnelling. It sounds like a dangerous kids toy to me, but I'm all for brain maintenance stuff. They can sell 'em at Home Depot."

In her mind it was as if I (the poet, the man) could just simply dry up, vanish, implode, or dissolve at any given nanosecond. But here I am.302050825252,.302050825253. And maybe this epiphany she may have been having is not a good one. Maybe I should not dissolve. Sort of the opposite of living. So hard to figure these things out, what with introversion and all.

"I don't want to think about the fish today, Cate."

"So we won't then. Save that for another time. I saw a great review in the paper today—or was it an interview?—about a new reading series starting up. Maybe you could read there."

"Cate, I keep finding silhouettes of reason, notes with 'might wanna eat a girl and think some apple sauce is comin' by' on them. Someone may be remixing my vocal cords and, like in the bowels of batter, in the bowls of irony, a misfortune cookie is a-coming for me. Something. Maybe that's the poem."

"Let's drink tea," Cate goes.

I am staring at the note with all the bravery of a Hollywood astronaut in front of a green screen.

"Charles?"

The morning is nearly over. I had plucked fresh herbs from the garden around nightfall—nothing else to do—and despite my own sense of inactivity, I had already left a trail of disorder for her to find me under: plates, cookbooks, indiscriminate papers, avocado pits, ginger root remains, clothing, socks, peppermint cuticle cream, Post-it notes, torn envelopes, and rice cake corners. Not that these things are all piled high and I'm at the heap's bottom—

I should get on with it. There are leftovers in front of me.

"I can't finish this calamari, Cate. The appliances hum in this preordained mutation and have no spirituality. The furnace, the oven, even the humidifier balk and riot me. I feel brittle. Weakness Wednesday will continue here in Maudlin. Oh, yes it will."

As Cate stares in terror, I realize it would be the perfect time for a musical montage break. No such luck, I continue my sermon of the mentally thwarted.

"Nailed each day, my grocery list along the stomach lining of my mismanaged guts, the handwriting rotting." Is that a poem? I wonder. "Nevermind, Cate. Malfunctioning. Old data. How I long for convivial tears in my steelplated psyche, ward and all."

"Want honey in your tea?"

"Sure." Unrelated, I consider myself the worst published poet in all of Maudlin City.

"Want me to put it in the fridge?" Cate suggests. "The tentacles?"

"Yes." I sip the tea. "Oh, speaking of tentacles, have you heard from Daniel?" I begin to pace by the mauve curtains. Drawn tightly, they are dark and thick, making the front room awfully dark for a sunny day. Making me concentrate on Cate's answer.

"Cate?" She doesn't answer me. Daniel's her tutor buddy, but I'm convinced he murdered a bunch of people with his extremities about two months ago. The police have no leads.

"What's wrong?" I ask. I can never tell with Cate from one second to the next what she's thinking or talking about.

"Daniel left for Spain. He's never coming back. It sucks."

"Sorry." It sucks? He sucks. Sucks the life right out of innocent citizens . . .

I want to give her the story I wrote about Daniel in Spain and everything, why he had to go. Instead I read her another story idea I have: maybe to change the subject?

"How about, like, a sexy story, for one of those anthologies with the log cabin on the cover and a muscular were-wolf holding a bottle of wine? The hotel mattress sighed uneasily at our bodies piled on top of one another, 'Bring out your dead,' she said, filling up our plastic cups of dwindling ice. The rest is a blur of pink, red, and teeth: lover's spit and treacherous sweat."

"Maybe work on the squid poems," Cate suggests, "if you can find them."

The mauve curtains would soon be opened by one of us and the weather would begin again. Life would be lit correctly.

You could call it poet's block. Then again, I am not much of one. Despite a debut collection, *Communication for the Damned*, two readings, and no less than four Maudlin blog mentions, my work doesn't readily appear on any poetry radar in the city, let alone country. The city itself is a rejected poem, named after my aunt.

The phone rings. It sounds funny, queer, as though hooked to an old-fashioned garbage disposal. Or iron lung.

"I'll get it," Cate says.

Like emergency surgery organs in ice, Cate is now carrying bits of my still-ringing phone toward me, placing them next to the bits of my answering machine, which she had fished out of the garbage. Everything is kept together by a long green cord, a sort of telephone artery that can never be fully severed from my bright life.

How I landed Cate as my intern is a marvel in itself. She had answered my ad from a posting at U of M's English department: "Assist a poet in putting together his second book and other literary lifestyle duties."

In a matter of minutes she'd be free.

"Cate, how's this opening stanza: We awoke in each other's horror-gaze like two malicious wedding-cake action figures, two crisp morgue couples, mangled beyond recognition. Our breath stank of cigarettes, rum, and each other's blurry DNA."

"Charles, the person on the answering machine keeps saying, 'STUPID STUPID STUPID,' over and over again."

"I see. That's specific. Causality aside, what's the overall mood then?"

"Okay, here's the message, part of it anyway. I guess the tape is pretty worn out on this thing."

"Who is it from?"

"I have no idea." Cate is hot-wiring the gear, manipulating the machine with a pencil.

"Maybe it's my editor?"

"No idea," Cate goes, "but whoever it is has disguised their voice somehow." She chokes for a moment. "I believe a trance song is playing in the background, but it could be your coffee maker percolating, or switching on, when it was recorded; both machines share the same outlet."

"Sorry about all this. I know it's technical."

"You should think about getting a machine that isn't older than me."

The voice gurgles gritty through my small, impotent speakers; I know full well who is leaving the message, so I begin tiptoeing into my subconscious to gnaw on the candy-orange grocery-store mechanical bull of my childhood. It's a calming technique I mastered over the course of my varied and elaborate emotional air raids. I chew and chew on its imaginary orange bull ears; the bull vibrates with the memory nickel I drop into the blue coin box beside its feed bag. The plunk comforts me: the nickel in the machine makes a nice, clean sound, a swell ruckus massaging my little life. The nickel spitting up, reinserting itself, spitting up, reinserting, replaying the ride. I stand up, tipping my chair over in the process.

"Oh God!"

Cate runs down the hall from the kitchen. "Charles, what's wrong?"

"I have heartburn! I am drowning in a tide of pure devil

lemonade!" I go. "I can't live another second. I demand wood wasps come and mistake me for a treasured wooden monument moments before my big reveal. I demand wood wasps drill holes inside me, mimicking high-octane surgeons high on airplane glue!"

The voice on the machine continues: "Charles, ah Charles, yes, well, you are criminally vulgar. I only forgave you because I needed you so much. Maybe it's better to be lonely than have this. Liar! You'd have to do something really brave to overcome my disgust. But go ahead, put on another mask, it doesn't matter if it's you I love anyway because you don't feel reality."

"Cate, when was this message left?"

"Two hours ago. Can I go at noon?" Cate is chewing her nails.

"So, at nine this morning? Okay. Yes, thanks for all your work; I hope you have enjoyed your internship."

"No, not really. I'm not putting it on my resumé."

"I appreciate your honesty."

As she prepares her things, I know Cate can hear my tiny whimpers grow, and for a single moment she stops. She approaches me, in my weak pajama theatre, a sad, uncombed, black-coal state, puts her hand on my shoulder and watches the intense reflection of my puzzled face in the computer screen.

"Cate, murderers are running through sprinklers

tonight. On Maudlin's sick soil. They're running through in sad technicolour with steak knives slicing playfully through the sprinkler streams, those prison lines of water. They're practising, like those are arteries in wait."

I look at the deformed answering machine she holds in her hand. The wreckage is too much. Burbling coos and beeps swirl and warble; hiss and static come to a boil on the playback as—"Charles, whenever you talk to me, you sound like a television commercial. Then you make me wear your cock as though you don't even want responsibility over that as well. Don't write me a poem instead of speaking. Don't spew out lyrics instead of committing to me. You can't even love love."

In the basement washroom, sensing the onset of personal decay, I brush my teeth with an apoplectic vision and floss until my gums bleed. "That's right, bleed!" I go.

I've got to become a real person. I hear the phone ring; I listen to Cate's voice.

"Cate, was that someone?"

"No, wrong number. Someone named Jim looking for Shawn."

I go immediately to the mauve curtains. I am weeping and Cate holds me somehow, moves me to the couch where I melt until the weight of my pain is too much and she replaces her lap with a pillow. Ever since that April evening not so long ago, when I had mentioned to a group of Maudlin City poets how I'd killed a pentapody with an old boot in my living room, no one in the poetry community would speak to me. That's not why I'm weeping.

"I just want someone I can write a straightforward poem about," I go, clutching several scraps of paper, "without having to bait the trap."

"Creepy times." Cate says, moving bits of her fire-red hair out of her eyes. "You, ah, want some help?"

"I mean, I'm not asking for a lot, not like vending-machine-selection easy, but still, relatively straightforward. Just allow me to have my moment, something like, 'Soft breasts were soft; skin, tender skin, come in; scent captivating, vapour chasing, kisses, warm kisses, warning me along her sleeping face.' "

Cate rolls her eyes. "Gross."

Cate looks down at the hazardous sorting ahead of her: a series of poems in red ink printed on baby blue paper jostle her eyes. She reads the first poem and is immediately repulsed by the memory that she has, in fact, already read them.

"What about these, uh, vasectomy poems, Charles?"

"I hate those."

"Me too."

"I should edit them," I suggest.

Cate does not blink when she says, "Or burn them." She flaps the pages. "All of them!"

4.

Thrown in the furnace of what experts would call "romantic burden," I can only imagine how freeing it is to flee me. To be a poem trapped and contorted, all bonsai-tree cruel—it's just so sad. People are not poems. Thank God Amnesty International doesn't know about me.

"Cate I'm looking for that poem about a shoulder of lamb. It may be called 'The Romantic Furnace.'" I leaf through a stack of paper. "No. Not in this pile," I say.

I notice some flies, several high-flyers perhaps three days away from death, circling a light fixture in vulture mimicry.

"One time she was talking about wanting to shoot," I go, "from, you know, down there—to spray. She asked me if I felt it, if she sprayed."

Without movement, I am storming the castle, wading in the tirade of my own itemized anxicty.

"You know what I mean?"

Cate is silent.

"But how can I write about that in a poem?"

"Why would you write about that?" Cate asks, looking at her boots. They still look sort of new: soft black leather with a round silver buckle on the side. Authentic motorcycle boots, the same kind her mom wore.

I hold a pen. "He was in the middle of writing a terrible poem," I say, pretending to type my odd sermon up, "and frustrated beyond belief at *Weak Paddle*'s submission policy, he pounded his fist into his substandard desk in frustration. He said 'frustration' so many times, he felt substandard, he debased his goals, he punted, and he shrugged in embarrassment."

Cate waters a plant. I stand up and walk toward her. "Did I ever tell you about my uncle, the one who left me this house?"

"No," Cate says, sounding almost proud.

"Oh, I could tell you about it, since you're in it and all."

I can tell Cate wants to laugh, but she is a very strong character.

"After he died I found a box of chocolates."

Cate laughs. "Sorry, I thought for a sec you said 'after I died.' Like you . . ."

"A box of chocolates and two *Playboys* under the couch," I say, not letting Cate steal my thunder.

"Oh. Well, that sounds fun. Not a bad way to go."

"I don't think that's what killed him. You never can tell though. Expiration dates and all."

Cate's desire to leave is great. I read her something, "Listen to this, it's so confusing. WEAK PADDLE SUBMISSION POLICY: We will respond to your query slow as malaise, ensuring our powdered wigs don't fall from our extremely important skulls. Please format your poems with standard translucent Maudlin poetry finish, available from any major art store or typesetting software store. We prefer 20 lb bond paper to the slum printer paper most magazines accept. Also, we require a standard 0.8" indentation on the top and bottom of your text."

"You need me to mail something?" Cate asks.

"These guidelines are atrocious. *Ben Hur* had less detail."

"When's the deadline?" Cate asks, carrying bits of wire and parts of my phone. Half-eaten appetizers begin to broil in the sunny kitchen.

"When I write poetry," I go, "I feel as though I'm stealing the words from the mouths of people who have never, ever lived."

Cate is trying to keep me on course, "When is the deadline for this contest you're entering?"

"Deadlines don't concern me, Admiral Cate. It's the calls for submission sock hop itself that tires. They're asking for five to seven poems with themes that include 'product-based consciousness with a focus on nonlinear didactic resonance from pedestrian residue, and the voice must attribute longing and have a POV in the first-person consumer.' "

"Well, what do you have so far?"

"Alga rhythm arthritis tennis elbow quantum phys-ed digesting scalded meat by the bucket basement grope door still open peppering steak fevers distracted by tempting dessert menu paper cuts long lanky frame lemon squeezed on the hour on every hour adding lemon on every hour."

"That makes no sense," Cate says, digging around in her jacket pocket.

"That's just a cover letter," I go. "Okay, I'm joking."

Cate makes a strange half-camel face. "Oh yeah! I forgot about this fax." She is waving a piece of paper at me. It's always this way. Hand me the piece of paper and I'll have the heart attack.

"So you know this Terry guy?" she says, looking exactly like an intern reading from a bad script on one of those senseless Canadian dramas. "Says he wants you to come to the studio to record the voice-over you wrote for this dance video thing." Cate lowers the fax from her face and looks at me. "That's good news."

"Yeah, he owes me a favour, that guy. So when do I have to go?"

"Anytime. Says they liked the feel of your script."

"It felt good. Like yogurt."

"Anyway, they want to show you some clips from re-hearsal, then, you know, you'll record while watching the clips, I guess."

"Sounds like a one-way trip to Snuff Film Island. I like it."

Cate leaves the room but, before doing so, places the fax on the table near me. I am pleased with myself, but only temporarily. The thought of fish fraud hasn't plagued me in a few days and for this I'm grateful. My job at the beach is going to get busy, but nothing like working directly with people like this voice-over deal. This might be a good out-let for me, a type of rehabilitation.

Cate asks if there's anything else to do for the day. I can't think of anything so I unchain her. She makes gestures and packs up her things as if she's putting down a giant military rifle with the bladed tip full of papers and leaves in a quiet hurry. My mind races, I'm running on empty; my stomach is hungry, but I know the idea of cooking is a tremendous storm I cannot weather. Instead I'll prowl around the couch cushions of my dead uncle's house and hope for the best. Cate will not be my intern forever. Soon I'll have to gain the courage to read my own faxes, open my own emails, and format my own cover letters.

In the days that follow, I'm immersed in recording at the studio, working at the beach, and writing a story about Cate riding a wintry bus to the airport with a mini television on her lap to say goodbye to Daniel, the boy she won't tell me about. Or maybe I just don't listen. Either way, this trident focus offers insights into my elastic abilities I would have never otherwise known.

I love the way my voice plays back in the studio and how excited the technicians are when I get it right. I love the beach as well, the jean shorts and parade of perverse courtship I witness like a vagabond shipwrecked in the middle of a civil war, taking a make-out break with a sketchbook. In the story I work on for Cate she is watching a nature program on a small television while the slow bus makes its way through the teeming blizzard to the airport. She is fidgeting with things in her silver purse, and she is nervous because she feels like she'll never see Daniel again.

I leapfrog from project to project to project until the back-knees of my jeans are permanently creased and stand on their own like a loyal action figure left in the rain.

5.

It's late July. I'm lonely and cannot sleep. Again, I find myself by the lake; it's very late, my voice runs over the soft part of night that I've made my own, this sort of creepy nook: a tiny patch of grass before the beach and shore. It hits the water just so.

Maudlin's soupy promenade and piers (once honestly dedicated to amusement, searing the wages from good folks who had saved them with sly, vitriolic patience), is now a false edifice, corroded by goading condo parasites, home to the working-class pigeons (relics of animal programming), urban squirrels, and seagulls. The grounds have been recast; ugly swan-weeds have risen up in one broken-boned nuisance, assigning an uneven shadow to the shore after immense wind. The sadness hangs silent in advertisement, the evidence of labour gouged in dense outlines, ghastly in intricate detail as future clone-buildings are readied. It's far from the long, weaving, maddening crowds of briny pleasure. This cold Maudlin sun, the high-octane music belting from car stereos, the rattle of the street cars bristling past the skeletal remains of the astronomer's museum, the souvenir windmill, with its large wounded rudders and its door in basic chains, the abandoned horse stables, and all the wood gone wrong.

Cate answers her phone. She's barely awake, God bless her.

"You know, I'd feel like a true stranger away from here, Cate. I suppose I'm *real* Maudlin."

"What do *you* want? What would make you happy?"

I don't know what to tell her. "Something will come up. Maybe I need a vacation. Or to plant a garden."

"Charles, I gotta go," Cate says, slurring. "I'm so tired."

I'll describe some of my amazing peripherals and visual accruements here along Maudlin's beach: with vacant strides a couple saunters toward the only bench that clenches itself along the sick lake's strict and dismal contours. A set of high beams is extinguished as the last trail of cars peels from the sparse parking lot. The couple breathes melodiously and in sync, extracting fresh air from the supply. The midnight silhouettes of water outlines are superficial but stark. In its detail the dead eels or carp, the crime scene dental floss, cracked plastic medicine bottles, and chewed plastic soldiers may as well not exist. I like this time of year, all the lilac and cattle.

They are undressing now: one muscular limb for one sultry limb—matching skin—shifting and trading each other in the company of night's slutty tongue. Quivering along with them, the glistening liquid exaggerates, shrinks, and jostles in its lakey border. Poorly postured trees and a row of rocks and lumpy hills frames the shore. I pop 12 mg of Soderiaz. Tonight, along a manmade trail of inflected cement, the figures absorb one another: shadows, spit, and all in a similitude of touch, the flow of nature's harsh routine.

The bench is warm with midnight afterglow while their heads sink into one another and become a clump of gnawed clay. A defining system is at work here; dirty birds finger the water with beaks and toes, picking bugs from a lavish buffet.

Morning comes and I've slept through the night in my car. Just enough time to freshen up at the coffee place and set up for nine. You see, this is my new cover. Selling oils, lotions, and water on the boardwalk. How noir is that? This hot morning is day one of my eleven shifts in a row: the boardwalk and sun lotion; the tortuous bikini-clad rollerbladers blurring past my dark, sappy eyes, ass swirls, camel-toe-clutch submission holds, tummies beaded, glistening wet.

Cue Beach is way, way east of Maudlin City. It's a

neighbourhood in development: sand, sand, sand, tennis courts, new bling stores for beach moms, fine antique stores, a racetrack, a new eighteen-screen mega Cineplex, an Olympic pool erected in the mid-twentieth century, concert parks and parkettes, and many middle-class restaurants, both chains and independents.

Setting up each morning at 10 a.m. (or, if I have an afternoon start, 2 p.m.) consists of a folding table, two cases of suntan lotion, and at least six-dozen bottles of water that I keep stashed in municipal ice. The beige plastic table comes right to the edge of the boardwalk in the sand. I also bring along plenty of notebooks and writing instruments. I stare at the polluted waves, dreaming of buoyant impossibilities.

If I'm lucky, a set of girls comes and asks for directions. It's creepy, selling lotion in the slutty sun to the half-naked, but like the goldfish gig, it's a cover. I smell their aromatic brevity before they twirl and blur off—smelling their plastic straws—all lips and—

"It's my creepy job," I could say: all day long, or not. I daydream about the possibilities, while trying to piece together Maudlin's sinister plot. Garden shears move with angry vindication. Seagulls and crows cut through the vilified, bleak quadrant of sky—the strengthening grey quarter-sky from the southwest.

I watch diehard fishermen troll Maudlin's dirty-bird

lake for skunk fish. That's what I call them. "How's da skunk fishin' going boys?" That's what I mutter, imagining myself the kindred town-relic type: insane, with a grey beard and liquid rust for snot.

On my break I become the beach, hermit-crabbing along a sunny cross-section of sand and, oh boy, do I swat the flies and vermin that calculate my every move. And when I fall asleep for a minute or two, I feel heavy and rusty. The sound of the waves draws time over me like a net, and the aggravating flies and squawks, they too represent their own time-spanning properties. They bite me. They headache me. Land, crawl, blur the air before me with black zig backs and the black zag backs, and sometimes the mad dagger being buried speaks loudly and shipwrecks me in back pains, and sometimes I have to pack it up early.

Now, however, nighttime, all stalker; I feel like a mad dagger, a mad, dull dagger being buried slowly by thoughtful grade-school kids, the sort that would have a dagger to bury in the first place, or might want to bury a dagger. This daydream, parked at night, disturbs me to no end. It knots my guts into several thick lumps.

6.

"Hi Sailor," she goes.

I am all squinty. The sun controls me and pushes me down with its annoying, stinking thumbprint. I meet Robin Beedie one Tuesday afternoon at a record store on Bleecker Street. It's the busiest store on the strip.

"Hey again," I go.

"Oh hey. I saw you selling on the beach yesterday. You look sad a lot."

"That's me."

It's one of those things; you bump into someone enough times, you're in the same places, you're both people, and it builds like a current. She's an extra in the short dance film I'm voice-overing, over and overing. We've talked about this fact already like six times. We use words like "rehearsal" and "shot list" and "storyboard."

Then, at a party two days later in the fashion district:

"I re-wrote something for that scene you're in, in the washroom."

"Cool. What are you up to this evening?"

"That is so crazy you know Terry," I go. "Crazy" is one of Terry's words. "Well, I'm here, then that's about it. I don't have plans really. It's early still. Anyway, who do you know here?"

"I know them from the record store," Robin goes, pointing and inhaling to a couple of boys in plaid shirts and tight pants.

"Right," I go. What else can I say? I'm sort of drunk now.

"Terry taught me how to steal bagels from the grocery store; you just carry them around in the plastic bag and eat them." she says, her dimples stapling through her cheeks with unrelenting pressure.

I can imagine Terry, the human leopard, slowly selecting mustards and trolling delicatessens with the facial tension of an architect, putting the last pompous tree beside a parking lot, crunching his face into infinity, like a good leopard does. Terry is a mustard leopard. I don't want to talk about him; I'm more interested in Robin's green evil-forest eyes and tiny shorts. Her arms are like celery and she looks badly drawn, paper-thin, and like she bathes in Mr. Noodles. Her eyelashes are extremely dark, her eyes, like I mentioned before, are evil-forest green. To me she looks like a wet spider, one constantly waiting to be let into your house, you know, to use the bathroom or to borrow a towel; she's always on the other side of the mail slot, grinning sickly each time you creak the thing open.

The next time I see her at the store she greets me with an explosive smile. I think someone she loves is behind me or something, maybe a large raccoon dancing. She has cut her hair extremely short and is wearing a bandana around her neck. Her friend Chelsey is there and we're introduced. Chelsey has the largest eyes on the planet and an infectious laugh. Robin introduces me as someone who worked on the video. "The one I wasn't in," Chelsey goes.

Robin signals for a change in the mood. "We're going for drinks, me and some friends, wanna come?"

Chelsey has big brown hair, a tiny nose, and looks like she's always about to giggle or burst into hormonal tears.

"Sure," I go.

And this is how I begin to balance an angry tidal wave and the rod of lightning shaped like a hissing tongue. I wonder if Cate is still sleeping. I haven't even thought about poetry for, like, four days. My legs hurt from standing. I want to stop miming along through the universe.

"All my girlfriends will adore you," Robin says, making sure Chelsey is not in earshot. I would like to believe her; I would also like the pain in my ankle to leave my body and fall into an anthill like a pear slice.

Less than an hour later and we're all drunk.

"It's my birthday. I'm turning . . . next week, guess how old I'm turning to be?" Chelsey stammers.

At the Marie Street bar I grab her because we're done smoking and she's getting excited about her birthday. I am out of breath when I take her from the dark patio area into a bit of light. I throw her under it like an X-ray; I squeeze her arms and look into her kiddie face intensely and, taking into consideration her question, say, "Twenny?"

She tries to smile, but I've got her face all squished. "Twenny-one," Chelsey goes. She's all blue-eyed and tiny nosed, beautiful bomb of brown hair and almond skin.

I release Chelsey and she swishes outside, back to her gang of nicotine squirrels. In three minutes I go and try to make Chelsey-plans, you know, cook her dinner or something, maybe a dinner party. She says nothing when I ask her. Robin is nodding behind me. Chelsey says maybe next week. Now we're all splitting up to go to various relocations, separate ways, and Chelsey's white denim jacket dips east and left and I'm lodged on a dark street, feeling a wash of wind and night's accruing eeriness up my back.

Re: audition now for the chance to dance *for the rest of your natural life*. Do you want constant ass-shakes? Show details 5/15/_ Reply yes clothing of course. Tons of my friends, well, not friends but (4) are in it along with about 16 others. You have to dance and you are also given a turn filming stuff too. It's a mockumentary. So what kind of job do you have? I am desperately in need of work. Charles. CLICK FOR RELATED CONTENT Police: Girl killed in dance party heist gone wrong, the unanswered text messages . . . nightclub rejects responsibility . . . Victim's mother fights for Kimberly, seeks justice. I do not enjoy nachos and beer. I once got drunk with philo kings in 1994. You were 2 or 11 months old. SHOW QUOTED TEXT sorrie yr dead RIP SHOW QUOTED TEXT The Internet is a galaxy unto itself. People must know the hazards that can happen before interacting with strangers and they must stop. "Get the fuck out, I swear to you now, if you don't get out of here I'm going to drill a hole in your cheek and tie you to a truck. I'll cut off your fingers and seal the stumps with harsh weather-treating sealant or varnish." They carefully manipulated a young girl's insecurities, and she died as a result. They denied sending warning messages. Michaels was charged with one count of conspiracy and three counts of accessing protected computers without authorization to get information used to inflict emotional distress on the girl. "This was a tragedy

that did not have to happen," sources say. Jim wrote some
of the messages to Kimberly, and Shawn's disappearance
frightens the group. Thinks there's a greater evil out there.
They just "needed another body for the third prop coffin."
To attend the dance party. To have fun? Get drunk? Was
put in coffin took drugs found in park with rope around
neck asphyxiation suicide. No rope. No asphyxiation. She
hit her head; it was just a necklace she was wearing. There
was no necklace; it was a string with a key on it. Someone
tampered with her before police came. Jim said he saw
Shawn write a mass email to everyone, all high, about the
world being a better place without them, that they were
the "end of the world girls," that they would do a "dance
with death" at Frisk and it would be amazing. The idea
was to make a few grand. There was a fight over the money. The message was supposed to shock people to show
up to the event and get in the prop coffin, like Robin and
Crystal. Jim thought it was safe. "I think we were trying to
get her angry, I thought she wasn't going to come." Friends
say Kim came across as this wild child but then she could
be really sweet, etc., and that she was into painting. "She
was nice, not a mean girl, she was popular." Did she have
secrets? Like a stripper who changes her persona? We
all knew she lived in a small town with her mom and dad
and sister and worked at the library—exploited the frivolity
of alcohol, music, and fashion industry as tools for self-

destruction. The message was cribbed from a Ted Bundy victim: "*I escaped by the skin of my teeth. When I think of his cold and calculating manner, I shudder.*"

hurdy gurdy man

When the truth gets buried deep
Beneath the thousand years of sleep

Time demands a turn-around
And once again the truth is found

Awakening the Hurdy Gurdy Man
Who comes singing songs of love.

—Donovan (verse by George Harrison)

part two land of a thousand dances

Mourners laid flowers outside Leatherpalm's Siko night-club Friday as authorities raised the death toll to 19 from the blaze that ripped through the venue as revellers celebrated Victoria Day weekend. More than 120 people were injured early Thursday morning at the nightclub in the town's lively Ekko district, a thronging entertainment hub frequented by locals and tourists, in a grim start to the holiday weekend. "Of the injured, 63 remain in hospital with 13 in intensive care units," Chantal Simphoan, secretary of the emergency service headquarters, told reporters. The blaze apparently broke out after a fireworks display at the club.

1.

Someone is humming over the loquacious rustle of glasses, skirts, and couch shuffles. Fuselage gluc lies hard along the coffee table in lethargic, prehistoric rivers. The pithy computer screen glowers on its makeshift desk of phone books and plastic milk crates. I search on Robin's computer to prove a point: that the director had wanted someone else to do the voice-over, but when he couldn't offer them the money they wanted, came crawling back to—

A voice-over actor who didn't want the job began the thread. I discover the online proof. I do a bump off Robin's CD case. I find the message board online, a thread now six weeks old. One of three windows open on Robin's computer. And the basement smells funky and temper-tantrum music oozes from weak speakers, sounding as though rats have chewed the wires; some of the creatures have been electrocuted, rotting and perfuming . . . the heat and stink of garbage . . . night crickets . . .

"Can I bum a cigarette? Fuck . . . what time is it? I have to work in the morning," words and breath fossilize along the mould, landing on the grit . . . down the hall, the laundry room and its soaked carpets with high bleach content . . . white bread sopping it up casually.

"Here it is," I go. I stop the cursor and it blinks in front of the juvenile V/O, written by me, posted by the desperate director when it looked like I was not going to work out—but I did. The voice-over gig stirred up some local voice actors in the community:

Jean128: I wrote my objections to the website that posted this one:
Sex appeal.
Lust dungeon or sexual paradise?
We're all on the prowl.
We're all here to score.
It's time to play.
Nightclub party.
Retro party.
Space party.
Spring break party.
Our cameras take you on the dance floor;
as for our dancers they'll take you somewhere you've only dreamt of . . .
Intrigue . . . desire.

Vanity forms a sweaty queue. What are you going to
wear?
Steamy . . . toxic.
Touch yourself. Touch others.
Get dressed. Get undressed.
Hey, you might never leave your house again.
So call the gang over and get fictional . . .
Now for the first time ever the story of a girl, a boy
another girl, and another boy, a song and a dance
floor in one epic, epic saga.
Jean128: And it pays 100-250. This is the second time
I've seen it posted. The first time I just deleted it. Maybe
they didn't get any takers from the first post???? This
time I am voicing my opinion. OKAY. I'll get off my soap-
box now.
Walco26: The rest of it aside, I must say the last line of
the script is pretty darn funny.

New bodies have formed and swarmed Robin's basement, which for the last few weekends has been priority
destination for me. I'm bound to find poetry, bound and
gagged, under the couch cushions, stuck to some girl's
ass; and there is this new duck, this ducky girl with coily
black hair and chocolate-bunny eyes who is louder than
bombs. We're all bombed and afterwards, after the trickles
and ounces have spectrally fled after feeding off my pores,

dying in a tangled constellation too quick to take down to connect the dots, I go to Robin—half yawn—

"What's with Crystal?" I go. "She just goes on and on and on."

"Yeah, that's Crystal. She rambles. But I adore her," Robin concludes.

This nauseating parlance is now standard practice with Robin. She tells me about Crystal: her affair with the married professor, her recreational use of roofies.

"You mean she does it with basketball players?"

Robin doesn't laugh.

The words come and go, week in, week out: nauseating, not because they are nauseating, that's a different issue, not for me to say, but the drugs themselves create a dialogue I am not in control of—this is a new government, running my body into oblivion, creating new legislation.

"So when's the wedding?"

"What?"

"You're all she ever talks about," Robin goes.

"Very funny," I go.

2.

Nearly night, Thursday. The pre-season game is on television in another room. We're all at Robin's place again, me and the extras from the film, and Chelsey, who didn't even know about the shoot until Robin and Crystal starting blabbering about it.

"I don't know, I think he's not into me anymore. Maybe I blew my chance last time I was home."

"Chels, how do you take your tea?" Robin asks. She drops the tea bags into a steel pot, the boiling water pluming through the small kitchen, the whole moment climaxing in a gentle brown lab dye.

"He didn't even call to say goodnight," Chelsey says, scratching her behind, sidling up to Robin. She catches me catching her. "What? I had an itch."

"Michael?" Robin confirms. Chelsey nods.

Nasal drips and breathing . . . sniffing . . . a bit of coke still hard in crummy balls across the plastic case; similarly, bits cling to our nasal walls . . . another baggie is hidden in the room. I sit down, landing a hand up the sides of Robin's extremely short shorts.

"Hold your head back, for the drip," Robin reminds me, pulling my hand for a moment into her inner thigh . . . releasing it.

"It's better," I nod, staring a bit too long in no particular direction.

"Better go get Chels," Robin says, sipping on the remains of some mixed drink that probably has vodka in it. "She's all on her lonesome." Robin's green eyes slither toward the grungy staircase.

Creepy in the basement, and then stiff ligaments lubricate, "I'll get her," I say, walking up the stairs, feeling every bit the scientist's goon, snooping the swamplands to fetch what I could honestly fetish as a temporarily ditched, a passed out, Polaroid, hurtling in chaos, hurting in chemicals, and, like her contemporaries, Chelsey appears to have the immune system of a golden retriever, an out-of-town drama student at Maudlin University.

I see the big, bulbous lids closed, her baby brown hair soft doe wet, and I nudge her on the patio, partially covered by an umbrella but—

Her first words are, "I'm wet." Not in the hot wet way. The time is 9:47 p.m., the temperature 71 degrees Fahrenheit.

"I'm here to carry you in."

Chelsey is just shy of 5'3", a bit of colour and curves to her, tiny-lipped, giant-eyed, micro nose (ski slope, Kewpie doll), and a round but firm behind.

"I'm okay," she says in a soft, drunk voice.

I'm in love with her now instantaneously. Her glance is permanent confirmation, as if a large wasp, as if a leopard, has bitten me, as if I'm dead in the water, as if I'm sick and asleep and her breathing next to me is the only panacea.

"Hey," Chelsey says

I inhale and lift her out of the wet plastic chair like a ruined wedding-cake decoration, torrid in the lonely dark. Down the stairs she holds onto my shoulder at crotch level (my eyes and face hover momentarily at her jean snap—it's eyeing me).

"I'm okay. I'm okay," she repeats.

And so I set her up in the one-seater in Robin's scummy basement only to be accidentally hip-checked by someone. And it's Crystal—loose canon, a couple of years younger. Crystal is elastic all over the room.

A loud, familiar clatter bursts from Robin's cheap speakers: "The story of a girl, a boy, another girl, and another boy, a song and a dance floor in one EPIC, EPIC saga . . ."

"Play it again," Crystal says, fluttering in her wedged undies on loan from Robin.

"Nice booty, bee-ach," Robin heckles, staring at the

skimpy spectacle Crystal provides us all, wriggling into a tight Hawaiian print dress, yellow-and-aqua-themed.

"Skank!" I hear Robin, who's laughing silently with tears in her eyes, pointing to the computer screen. "You can totally see your boobs!"

"Naw." Crystal cackles a long, mildly awkward laugh, as if partially electrocuted.

Robin sips on her booze and reloads the clip. "We must watch that again."

"Why's it so slow?" Crystal goes.

"Why you such a ho?" Robin says, swigging some con-coction.

"Tsk, tsk," goes Crystal. "You can't see them. They're itsy bitsy anyway."

"Well, the sides," Robin says, watching the clip on her laptop. "You can totally see boobage."

Robin's basement smells like hot summer ass. People wander up and down the stairs for cigarette breaks. Drink-ing, drugging, and grab-assing.

"Play it again, Robin!" Crystal coos, stumbling around in bruised legs. We all bash our fucking shins on Robin's lousy plastic wood decor.

"Skank!" Robin says. "You look all strung out, babes!"

"Well, you know, I'm with friends so, my theory is, take me home if you see me on the floor." Like Robin, these days Crystal's disposable income winds up in her nose—

into the maintenance of her self-sacrifices. She has fits of drama, offers her conditions up in song, in dress, in undress, and in performance. Crystal sees that I have put Chelsey on a chair and heads toward the washroom.

"Here we go again," Robin goes. "I think she's messed up about Allen and, of course, she and Chels are arch enemies."

Earlier in the evening, when Allen, who is both Crystal and Chelsey's ex, was chatting up Chelsey, Crystal locked herself in the bathroom. She is repeating the gesture now.

"I think that she and Chelsey and Allen had a cigarette outside."

"Yikes. That would be messy for all of them," I surmise.

It's entertaining, psychiatric, and cheap Canadian horror-film fun. It's also really hard to keep track of, like a sea of tuna flakes and vomit constantly falling into my eyes as I swim underwater. Robin fills me in on the petty details when we're alone. And when the details have surfaced, when the movies or drugs are in transition, she endlessly offers me lists of dirty deeds, performative in nature, curious, and occasionally speckled.

"When I was like twenty-two or something," I go, shifting my weight on the couch, "I wrote a terrible novel about a gang of middle-class hipsters who attempt to emulate a gangsta lifestyle. In the book the main character, named

Perry, gets gang-beaten by his ex-girlfriend's new sexual conquest. He's buried alive in a hole and it's covered by a windowpane and the rain comes down and everything. I wrote the whole chapter one night high on psychiatric drugs."

"Sounds like something you'd write," Robin says. "Anyway, that shoot was a blast, I banged a guy, Crystal and I got to make out on camera—it was grand."

The voice-over has become a fungus, a parasitic jingle for a non-existent product, from which I believe—no, from which I know, I will never fully recover. You see, when I'm not in the studio recording slightly different versions of the crap script, I'm here with the bodies. I've convinced myself of a landmine of truth: that I am madly in love with Chelsey. Ever since the encounter with her small, drunk, rained-on lips, half-asleep, buxom brown hair partially flattened wet, and me helping her down the stairs like a total murderer, just to plop her down into the one-seater while the rest of us listened to records . . .

Robin: what a spidery little tart. For me to describe her, this far along, shot list or not, you must imagine a sweaty phys-ed–type teenage girl, smoking, nervous, fifteen or sixteen, arms crossed, green eyes all squinty, big cheeks but real thin and gangly-looking, short, mangled brown hair—just like a spider. I mean, Robin. Do spiders have brown hair? Decent-sized tits, the kind you'd see in amateur porn; a pencil-crayoned cartoon, a malnourished, evil-intentioned spider, who sprawls and stares and silently gnaws away at every moment of conscious time with soft time-bomb lips.

"You want?" Robin says, nodding to the big fat white worm on the record sleeve.

"Sure," I say and lower my head.

I've never done coke more than once. I've never done coke every other day for a month straight. It's been a summer of this: hunting, feeding off each other's sweat, schedules, and dented auras. In the discount bin three years down the road, we'll find the double anniversary edition on DVD, prod at it with our hook hands, our glass eyes tearing, and somewhere on the bonus disc will be a regurgitation of this thought, this little drugged, drowned, and destroyed synapse defunct moment: "When I was a young lad, twenty or thirty years ago, I lived in a big, boring city named Maudlin with a bunch of young folks ass-deep in debaucheries, who clung to each other like stinking June bugs trying hard to outshine one another. There were drugs, sometimes cake, dirty sex, malicious betrayals, pregnancy scares, and twitchy vinyl grooves."

So back to the video. The video Crystal keeps making Robin play on her shitty computer—a rough cut of this voice-over and visuals are online right now. Crystal's got this small walk-on appearance where she lights a cigarette and kisses someone, and I swear they both separately seem to wipe something on another person's back or pants. I swear, watch the hand gesture. I'm sure it's supposed to be a sensual touch, but it looks like they're wiping cum on some poor girl's back or something. Robin has a similar cameo, but she's much more blurry.

So it's like this dying-out cadaver version of a wrap party in Robin's abject basement apartment, and we've all heard them going on and on about their crappy cameos playing their cracked-out selves right and real, and how they want to impress the agoraphobic director but he never shows up because he's allergic to seafood, and Crystal won't shut up from the bathroom about how she made the roasted vegetables, and she won't shut up, and when she does open the bathroom door a crack her pale face is all dyed in like a million splotchy gallons of red wine, and she's getting more and more naked, and I am screaming to her that the film wrapped up two days ago and YOU'RE STILL IN WARD-ROBE, and she's on her cell and whispering to Robin, so who knows what they're up to.

I look at Chelsey who is laughing without making sounds. Robin and Crystal are acting like they're watching the moon landing on television, but it's just their blurry asses shaking on the small monitor.

Chelsey mumbles something: "You guys didn't even have a line," she spurts, before passing out again.

Robin is arrow-headed with a sober expression that charges through all of us. "Speaking of lines, Crystal, Charles, shall we?"

Total numb-gum nightmare. Chelsey falls back into the one-seater, only to perk up later when she's woken by the noise of us snorting away. As we do more, Crystal won't shut up; she's an infomercial, a speaking-in-tongues, changing her clothes as often as her online avatar, as often as she repeats her shocking sexual policy: "Just take me home if I'm incapacitated, just take me home, we're friends." This is Crystal's jingle.

The coke makes her even more verbose, bad-actor verbose, prowling on the hem of insanity, her eye ducts twitching, mischievous thumbs in cab rides go through my jean belt loops, and it all ends in a nasty twitch—until the next summit of summer's hot rage. I've gone wild now; there is nothing beneath me.

"More Thoroughbred Than Clotheshorse"
By C.J. Haas (manuscript circa 199–)

Perry Oaltch wants to be in a gang. To run one. The only problem is he lives at his aunt's place and she doesn't really have room for him, so organizing things is tough. He has black hair. It's short. His sidekick, Keegan Keely, messed on pharmaceuticals, plays along. Keegan has dyed blond hair. Kessie Kohler is the girl, until one night she leaves Perry for Meklong, a rival gang leader. Kessie has short red hair; it used to be blond. Jimmy is a guy who always asks to borrow five bucks, so he's called Jimmy Jack Five.

One night Kessie and two of Meklong's henchmen pay a visit to Perry. The boys are Bunkie and Dinger; those are made-up names, but they like their names. They liken themselves to Beavis and Butthead. Dinger loves Radiohead and thinks the guitars are real wicked. Bunkie eats large bread rolls he keeps in a backpack.

The visit is physical. "This'll teach you for messing with Kessie. Don't call her no more or you'll get it, punk, you'll comprehend," they might have said.

One thing does happen for real: They take Perry to a park where they've already dug a hole in the ground. They toss him in. It begins to rain. Kessie tells the boys to put a windowpane across the hole and proceeds to fuck one of the boys on top of the window, with Perry watching, half-dead underneath. Kessie makes loud noises and her bare ass bangs against the wet glass. They break the window with their fucking.

The next day Perry comes up with a plan to take over a funeral home by sneaking into the makeup room—the embalming part where they prep the bodies—and taking photos of people partying with the corpses. The plan is to show the funeral director the photos and to blackmail the company for money lest they show the families what they did with the bodies before the funeral; you know, all poor taste, all you'll never get away with this. So the deal is for money and for a fake funeral for Perry Oaltch.

So Kessie is invited. The plan is, when the funeral begins, and they're all waiting for the ceremony, right, Jimmy, another gang member, will tell Kessie to follow him to the back parking lot where a hot air balloon will be set up. "Come on Kessie, I love you," Perry says. But Kessie takes a flare gun from Keegan, who has one in his hand 'cause he's the lookout guy, and she tries to shoot Perry or the balloon. She misses the balloon, but the basket hits some telephone wires and the novel ends with Perry being electrocuted and everyone getting on with their lives.

3.

The teenagers are sharpening their knives and their teeth, and drinking from the drainage streams outside my house; their ammunition is infinite. They are carrying bits of paper in their mouths. It's not like I've been shopping around my deranged oddly-fonted manuscripts to local fanged teenagers to see if they'd be into some literary roleplay. Anything is possible with enough Ritalin and iodine.

What are you reading, Shawn? Something about wood wasps. *Oh. Come for dinner? Crystal and I are cooking mussels.* Really? *Yeah, you inspired us.* Why? *'Cause you were talking about how they were your favourite thing so we thought we'd try and cook them. What's a wood wasp?* What do you think it is? Okay, sorry, wood wasps are these things that scientists are monitoring because of the way the species tunnels, right, so they think the methods are good enough to mimic with a robot, so they can use it for brain surgery. *What?* Not real wasps; they would die inside your brain. *They could colonize though.* You're missing the point. *Friday after school?* Sure. Time? *Sixish?* Sure. I'll read you some more about it: a new surgical robot bores into the brain like a wood wasp. Researchers hope that it can reduce the number of incisions needed to reach different parts of a brain tumor; it can crawl across the surface of the brain and then burrow in. Son of a smaller hero. Also, for about forty bucks you can buy a prop coffin made of cardboard. For seventy-five, one made of pine. The dimensions are 74" by 22" by 12" inside and it takes thirty minutes to put together. This model cannot be carried while occupied, so we should get another kind. We want something sturdy. *We?* Yeah. You can get this one component and you got yourself a fully functional coffin that you can not only carry but bury as well. We need it to hold people while suspended in the air.

part three
this *is* hardcore

Did anyone tell you that he was going to kill anyone? No. It wasn't like that. Me, Robin, and Kim were partying and Shawn and Jim were like, "Can you get inside the coffins?" I thought it was kinda funny. *When did you first hear about the coffins?* From Shawn, about two weeks before. *Before the night at Frisk?* Yes. At first, I thought it was a joke. Then I saw the coffins in the club hanging from these chains on giant hooks. It looked awesome and way freaky. *Who was driving?* No idea. *Did you know you were outside?* Not right away. *Let me rephrase: when did you know you were no longer in the club?* I was out of it. I just thought the tiny camera inside the coffin was showing my face, right, so I figured if I looked panicky, they'd let me out. *Did you look panicky?* No. I was crying though, I guess that's panicky. *When did you know something was wrong?* Just before the fall. I heard some screaming. *Then what happened?* I remember hitting the ground and thinking that I was falling, that the floor beneath me was gone and I was just plummeting. Then the top of my coffin cracked and I could see the sky. *Did you get out?* Not right away, I was worried that someone was holding a gun or something, waiting for me to poke my head out. *How long did you wait?* Hard to say. *Continue.* I was at the bottom of the hill looking up. I could see out of the crack in the lid. I opened the lid, and then I remember trying to stand up and falling down on my ass. *Then you passed out again?* I think so. *Was Shawn there?* You mean outside, on the hill? No, I didn't see him anywhere after the club. *Was he in the truck, do you think?*

1.

I'm not talking. The voice over is over. The images remain in my retinas—the extras: Crystal and Robin, still scamper around, howling in the heatful summer nights. The voice-over matches the shot list: girls in bathroom, girls lighting cigarettes, girls laughing in hallway. Two seconds, three seconds, four seconds. CUT.

Screen time. Chelsey laughing: "I bet they cut their dancing out, I can imagine it was bad."

The evenings and the winking, this evening and its glasses of ice water, becoming autumn, stepping out of a season's pink skin into dark orange, burnt almond.

A knock on my door wakes me; it is barely noon. A woman's voice says: "Charles, rise and shine," and I know it's Crystal and she's in my front closet or somewhere close to the stairs, near the telephone and oranges, and I must have left the door open.

"Fin is in," I tell Crystal as she slides her ghostly, unslept limbs into the sushi booth. She is facing east, me west, and the sun is coming at us from the south.

"Yummers," Crystal goes.

It's early November, still a bit hot, but people are wearing toques and stuff. Crystal is yawning: mouth snagged open wide on Pause, a glitch. She always does strange things with her mouth and jaw, the bones seem architectured by an abstract impressionist; like a hyperbolic cartoon character expressing fake anxiety, acting twitchy, or as if she's just drunk a potion that is supposed to alter her, and the physical symptoms kick in and, you know, she starts to stiffen and contort a bit, dance around horizontally along the repetitive technicolour background.

"How do I look?" Crystal goes. She's wearing a slinky floral print dress and bobby socks; her hair is twisted into a mammoth bun on one side.

"Like you'll be pregnant by 3 a.m."

The food comes.

"Mmmmm, I've had this craving for spicy salmon roll all week," she says, taking the tiny thermal green tea mug into her gremlin fingers.

I'm a sick carp on the inside, maybe the outside as well, who thinks he's a slick shark entitled to fuck and chew anything and anyone in his mangy path. Yes, my path is mangy. Wait till you see the blitzed-out pixie sticks who wind up in my teeth. I have no rules or regulations: I just feed and sleep wherever I want in a gratuitous education of major hedonistic skin-and-spit collisions. My appetite is infinite.

"My mom put five hundred dollars on my Visa, so this is on me," Crystal says.

We eat our sushi and get stuffed. Five-minute walk to her place where we have a drink—Jack Daniels. We do some Ritalin.

"I love that mermaid picture of you," I say, staring at her computer. She's upside down, blue background, her curly brown hair and puckered lips. "You look skewered."

"I have to work at 10 p.m. You wanna meet me after, at one or so?" Crystal says. "Come on Charles, later . . . we'll have tea, watch a movie."

"Maybe. I'll leave you a message."

It's the next day. I know because of sleep, rare sleep, and I didn't go see her. I passed out in my car. There was a plan to meet up early, regardless, and I feel both numb and calculating, a lumbering side effect unravelling like gauze from the new levels of locust pharmaceuticals chalking my blood. Soderiaz up the woozy creek that is my blood. Not to mention everything else. I'm coming from one confused entity to another, carrying the confusion bug with me, harnessing the standard weakness kit, a fucked-up

salesman showing little sign of fatigue. To mention everything else would require a tape measure, lost recordings,
muffled late-night takeout orders, and romantic sketches
done in God's likeness, on his drugs, about his children—
the ones I eat.

Some café on University Avenue. Crystal shows up
at 10:41 a.m., more or less, (her stellar jawline cutting
through a crowd of caffeine championing co-eds), and
keeps checking her phone. We ask each other how our
nights were and she's texting frantically. We have coffee
and chew the Styrofoam and squeeze each other's legs. She
tells me about how I should be worried about the boys
from the other night, especially the deejay with the girl-
friend willing to do anything for the chance she says. She
says something like this—I don't know, I'm not really paying attention to the details at this point, but I know the
coffee has put several holes in my stomach. The lining is
weak and I know I'm going to drown soon. My intestines
are covered in weak cheesecloth; I am certain.

"So, you know, all I'm saying," Crystal says, "I want to
be with someone who is nice."

"I see."

We go to her house. I think that I don't know this person at all. If this person can be defined by what she has
told me, then I feel like asking, but I don't ask, I don't say.
But that's all I am. A quick jot . . . thought . . . I am just this

flesh and bone, moving and walking and forcing muscles, Neanderthaling through each second of today. One day at a time. Two million days CE.

We take some Xanax. We smoke a joint. We drink tea, green tea, and watch streaming television on her computer, and eventually make lunch. We fuck. She smells good and I swallow each kiss and breathe hard. I monster her ass in bites. I conquer her neck. I bite hard.

"Let's go for a walk," she suggests after. I feel like an insane murderer.

Crystal is already layering hands clumped in mittens, neck covered in a snake of a knit scarf. She's looking at herself in the mirror. "I'm all mittens and dimples," she goes, and all I can think of is Chelsey in her thick, snoozy duvet, her miniscule dwarf red rose lips making sparse, fishy movements, her self-proclaimed "rump" hiding in the blankets, her make-believe eyelids freighted in a heavy lacquer . . . the soft, almost inaudible voice sleeping against her dense pillow, pouting cute with eyes still closed, wanting a kiss, a nose rub, a little love, a lick.

"Ready?"

Crystal's face slices me. Her kisses gut me. I keep her on her toes and well-stocked in asshole sadness. She's like a chemical dye showing up in supernova bloodstream X-rays like a crime show deal. I can't even really think now.

"Ready?" Crystal repeats and I'm following her bum

down the stairs. "Got your bag?" she asks and I guess I do because she looks at me quizzically and then says "Oh," a bit astonished.

Maudlin's central core shrinks behind us. The buses hiss, the wind is weak. Crystal puts her arm through mine. The buildings' darkness tapers into the sky. Yellow squares where some lights still resonate are the only real light being offered.

We've been walking for thirty minutes, sharing cigarettes and singing. Two boys run toward us in a blur of solid colour (and I soon discover—stubble and cheap cologne). I look at Crystal. Why are those boys stampeding? Where did you sleep last night? On a railroad track, bound and gagged, memorizing scream patterns, the rhythm of the track? This is the sound of regret and anger carried by sneakers along soil, awakening underground sororities (the stingy, reclusive comedy of soil scampers below the juvenile skid marks of left print, right print). Crystal steps back.

"So . . ." she says. I look back at the boys getting closer. "I dunno . . ." I say. "What should we—"

The hard metal slamming into the small of my back is real; I'm winded. A second blow lands at my upper spine, the knotted bone, you know, right at the top there, in between the shoulder blades, and that one just sends me reeling. Another blow—what is that now, a foot stomp?

I'm bound in a car. No soundtrack. No sound check. No second take. No voice-over or split screen. This is all *real time*.

I smell the city's malignant truths and entrails: cigarette smoke, car exhaust, watermelon gum, and sulfur. Wool on my face, the winter night air, the kind you suck up bravely before cowering indoors—all over me.

I know the car door opens because I feel the air on my feet, colder, and then another door slams shut. My ankles are clasped together; someone or some people are lifting me by the legs and shoulders. There is a hang time before I pile up and the earth catches me. I have landed awkwardly; this much is certain. On a root or part of a tree stump? The night is finished.

It has taken ten years to adapt this moment from the page. I always thought writing about this strange anti-fantasy, night in, night out, would prevent it from happening. Or at least prepare me. Shit. Dirt across my chest. A sort of devilish shout and smack in the face prompts this extemporaneous séance: post-coital cosmic vengeance, punishment for my co-ed ransacking in what can only be described—if I survive—as totally psychiatric reverse sex-crime roleplay . . . recreational . . . a crystal ball bong broken, delivering this brutal message in brutal misfortune. It's my misfortune, wrong turn. The way I barely move in the earth now is no different from six weeks ago, twenty years ago, ten, four. I'm a worm, a thoughtless worm with numb ends.

The story was simple: middle-class Perry Oaltch loses Kessie Kohler, tries to get her back, but she won't budge. One night, Kessie and her two male friends grab Perry from his sleep and take him to a park to scare him, burying him in a mock funeral, complete with rain and windowpane. The message: *Now You Know It's Over*. Priceless 1990s reverie. I honestly regret leaving even the slightest synopsis around in front of mixed company. People get obsessive ideas, rewired perceptions.

"Hold on," Crystal goes. She shoves a pill in my mouth, makes me swallow it. "Eat it, bitch," she goes, laughing with her inalterable grimace, reinforcing the cackling lava surrounding me. What the hell did she give me anyway?

In staggering detail I see Crystal's brown eyes ballooning out of her head. She's laughing as I'm swung; she counts along: one, two, three. Her legs move like scissors, her micro skirt caught up in the moment, the rain on her sweet bum skin, her panties now a deeper, cleaner, sharper blue, a light, wet blue, the way denim darkens when wet. And all this talk about colour isn't preventing me from— ouch—

I have exploded in the ground. I see the dirt. I smell it. My bones are covered in flesh, not the other way around. I join my life; my life has been a big corpse already in the ground. Just like Kessie and her gang of men did to Perry Oaltch in my dated manuscript, Crystal and her gang are placing the windowpane over my oozing form. It's a nice window, white paint slightly chipped, double-paned. I feel like I'm deflating, whatever they gave me—warble, warble, warble.

Crystal's face is wet and punitive. My face feels like a broken pomegranate, the glistening seeds begging for rain. Like Perry, I wait it out, convinced that this is just a phase I'm going through, a semi-carnality. I know what I have become. A senile old man becoming infantile again, drooling in a wheelchair at the beach. My archetype is not the male hero, but the perverse animal—I drop my popcorn so the short-skirted nurse has to bend over to pick it up.

2.

I put my hands under my head and assess my physical status: legs feel so-so, arms sore, back very sore, neck has some kinks. In the ground I see a miniature human, pacing, then sitting, then pacing. I try to focus on the dirt wall I've been admiring; I turn my head to the left and notice the microscopic person is saying "It's Shawn" into a small telephone. He also says "Crystal!" He moves slowly, this little worm named Shawn, he has light, waving hair and is wearing a docile red hoodie, which he's taking off to reveal a greasy undershirt. He wears blue cords. He tries to wriggle fully from the soil, pulling part of himself up using an exposed root. The longer I concentrate, the better I can hear his voice; I can hear the conversation in brilliant ground-surround-sound.

TRUTH! Itchy—very, very, ah dreadfully, ah beaded sweat on my brow. I had been on land and now I am in earth; but why will they scream in my face that I am mad?

Reporters? Students? No one? The itchy teenagers galloping through mayonnaise and carcinogenic altitudes on
my front lawn, and now my maggoty future; this disease
of life sharpens most of my senses—never diluting them.
Above all, my sense of hearing is raised like fever; I hear all
things in the city, here deep in the earth. How, then, am I
dirt? Am I this boy, Shawn, pacing back and forth in a wife
beater? Shouting?! Observe how healthily—how calmly—
I can tell you the whole story.

It is impossible to say how first the idea entered my
brain; perhaps it was through a biotechnical pre-forensic
wasp path; well, I mean wasp in mimicry. But once conceived, those scientists will justify their spending by giving mascots a kickback, and so this pain now in my back
and deep in my mellow bones haunts me day and night,
as if I've birthed a hideous babysitter who slits the throats
of unborn children. There is nothing discernible; it's too
dark to tell. We, the species that crawl and mite our way
through the relics and highways of life, are as passionate
as thoroughbreds.

I see him, half-boy, half-worm. Shawn. I can hear his
small lower-shelf voice, and he's on perhaps the tiniest
cellphone imaginable right here before me in the dirt,
coiled in the root and matter. Shawn leans into the phone,
half naked on his bed. I can make out that he's now in
his boxers or something and he keeps checking the time

on the small digital clock beside his bed. He's pulling out the steel coils from his mattress; he is twisting the pieces of metal into a noose of temporary connection, and then crumpling them into a discarded draft of a ball. He hears the click and knows his voice can be preserved for Jim to understand exactly what is expected of him. Jim is his best friend, seemingly; they've been friends since they first ran through each other's sprinklers with steak knives in their teeth one summer for a double-barrelled family barbecue performance.

Shawn begins: "This night is gonna rock. We just need to go over a few things."

"Sure, what are you doing at four?"

What Shawn wants to tell Jim is this: This uneasy feeling gets me around the neck, it roots itself deep, then rips out my pupils and eye ducts, and then Crystal is back saying I love you, and then she is back saying sorry I have been such a bitch.

You feel good, refreshed, renewed, the computer screen full of a cropped set of male green eyes makes you limp and weak, the scent of distant cologne and saliva-swallowing, anticipating some heightened reveal that you know will eventually discard you. You are Crystal. Shawn is the last thing on your mind. You bike to the grocery store, you smoke pot and listen to techno, and you live your life

beside a jpeg tacked up on a bedroom wall with masking
tape and your own sweaty dark pubic hairs . . . and then
you get a friend to take a picture of your bum . . .

As Shawn you feel disastrous, bloated, sick, scales out in
the sun as your antique stomach swan dives, as you twist
your body into a water-soluble pretzel. You come up from
the earth still knowing you no longer possess her. So what
do you possess—the feeling of hopelessness? You find a
handful of coins somewhere in the backyard of this anger;
you must have dug them up, so now what? Buy a boat? Sail
to hell? You look out the window; winter is dying, slowly.
Insects who were once ready to unplug their life cycle ex-
pose themselves to the slow corrosion of winter; they have
returned anew.

Crystal types on her computer, a roach in her mouth, and
tiny scribbles of cannabis pockmark the air as textbook
spines, crisp and fortifying on her desk, remain unopened.
I can see her doing these things too; she is a silkworm.

The phone rings.

"Hello?" she says, crooking her silkworm jaw, all green
and webby.

No one on the other end. She hangs up and continues to
seep deeper and further away from what was or is real. She
keeps digging with her soft brown pupils into the screen,

burrowing silkworm–like. Do they do that? Impossible to say, digesting, all of them.

"Look," Jim goes, "she's not going to phone, and you are not going to phone her." But I don't think Shawn's buying it—"I think you took it way too seriously. She's young, adventurous; you're not that way. Besides, she's pissed about Robin, seems only fair. It was doomed from the start."

Then I can hear Jim, who is like a caterpillar in the sense that he is thicker than the others, maybe he's a centipede, "I gotta go with my mom to pick up my sister. Listen, don't call Crystal."

I love the young people; I marvel at their energy, their desire to avatar and blink. Somehow, Shawn seems like a bad seed who will wrong the town soon. So I listen. I listen to them like they are ghostly silver thoroughbreds, galloping past the telephone wires.

Shawn keeps the eyes of vultures in his mouth, pale blue eyes with gelignite film over each one, and whenever his gaze falls upon me—oh wait, an announcement: *Maudlin City Public Health is advising the public to take precautions after a number of coyote bites in two north Maudlin parks.* He has never wronged me. He has never given me insults, or a paper. He has never been my paperboy; for his drugs I have no desire. I think it is his eyes, yes, these two light bullets I will describe to police: he has the eye of a vulture—with a film over it.

Now this is the point. You fancy me maudlin, a lunatic for all seasons, but you should not see me this way. You should see how painfully I proceeded with sore foreskin, with dirt in my fingers—and how disjointed they are. I'm cautious in telling you that it's not the young man Shawn who vexes me, but his wormy, gooey centre. The way I can see him gob along. I can see him and Jim, and the folds of their stomachs straighten and ooze or drip, flatten and bulge, and every morning, forever and ever now, I will feel them in my rotten soft apple dessert teeth. When the day breaks I will attempt to lift myself from this thoughtful death lounge.

"I haven't heard from you in a while," Shawn says, sitting in his dark adolescent bedroom, the only light coming in from the hallway through the crack under the door, from the life of his parents' activities.

"So, what's going on?"

His eyes are sunk behind their lids, a clamp, impregnable. His system slows all but the heartbeat and the feeling of his tongue repairing itself, ready for vanishing into regret.

"I've been busy," Crystal says, sighing. Her voice slows, a dying avoidance, a blender setting, churning through his arteries.

"How are you?" Shawn asks in an earthy but creaking voice. He lowers his chin into his chest; eyes still drown in the black.

"Look, last time we spoke things seemed pretty clear that we weren't—"

"Shut up! I made dinner for you. It took me almost six hours. And the last time you phoned me you indicated you were coming over. And you *never* came." Shawn pauses, glances at the video camera nesting in a heap of clothing. "Crystal, you said you were coming over."

"Listen to me. You never listen to me. I thought you were right for me, but you're too simple, you have a complex, dark side, but your other side is just too simple and I get so bored."

"Can't you just give it time? Can't we be together?"

"No. I'm not going to be happy with this. I feel trapped. I'm tired of dating people who just want me to be a projection of their fantasies and not mine."

Shawn's body ripples red, frame by frame, points on a graph, a dramatic pulse.

Crystal continues, "I am not going to wear a baseball hat for you and watch sports. I am not going to be your psychological mommy either."

"I'm confused."

"You are a little boy, so immature. I need someone—"

"Is there someone else?"

"Don't be silly," Crystal unstitches. "I'm not discussing my life with you. I need space."

I can't get out. I keep returning to the moist ground. I'm weak. The sound is a leak, her twinkling larynx. It's very late in the afternoon; the minor snow has completely thawed, and all that remains is a skeletal slush. My temporary bed is an even calm of muted browns and greens. The soil is firm, wet; the knitted grass is matted down, scarred by shovels or crowbars or whatever tools she deployed for my burial. The ground beneath me is moist and tepidly muting any hope of real texture, forms, or sway. The gristle of early winter listens to the symphonic mutters of cars, and these two voices also mutter in decibels.

Crystal is counting teddy bears on a childhood closet, the wallpaper never replaced. A week ago her fingerprints were magnets of hibernation, rubbing either side of Shawn's temples. And with her snake tongue pale blue from dyed drinks sliding out of the side of her mouth, she felt the draft from the window holler at her nape. Riding his stomach naked, she swam on him, elbows in the cold; settling down beside his chest she wriggled and whispered into his ear: Shawn's arms sprang to life with her touch.

Now, vacant and destroyed—

"Why are you laughing?" Shawn's voice is crisp and weak, loud and blunt, teeming in anxiety; his heart beats towards apoplectic certainty.

"I'm not."

"There is more to this. What were you doing all week? I called."

"*Living* my life. You're too suburban for me. Too simple." Crystal sips a glass of water, takes a handful of baby carrots, and chews orange. "So immature."

"So that's all?" Shawn watches his feet absorb the broadloom in the hallway, between the bathroom and the bedroom door, a moat of beige afterbirth, his lungs transparent in the hollow chirps of the empty house.

"When we're together it's like, oh God, he just wants me to be a lamp in his room."

"It's not like—it's not like that at all," Shawn retorts, a giant gesture begins inside, a boiling stream.

"Don't be annoying," Crystal goes.

"Why are you being so—so—difficult?"

"You are hurting me. I need to protect myself. You'll hurt me without realizing it because you're inexperienced and I'm too sensitive."

"Come over here. Now."

"No, and I'm not being difficult. I'm not. You don't give me anything."

"What have you been doing this week?"

"I told you, *living my life.*"

"What else?"

"Talking to this guy from White Orchid, going to Frisk.

I'm still interested in that."

"What guy?"

"I know you're upset, but it's what I want, and you'll have to accept it."

"How long have you been talking to this dude?"

"I told you about this, you just never listen. You never listen."

Shawn hangs up the phone. He opens the bedroom window, the light burns his eyes, the faint tones of whistling birds reverberate off the eaves, and an intriguing cloud begins to fill his vision. He enters the bathroom, walking toward the toilet, which sits underneath the window. In future sessions, he will sicken himself with inquiry; he will use her fantasies in an angry, hard, and physical way that makes Crystal feel yucky. This, she will explain, is his problem. He isolates sexual fantasy, separating his partner from the experience, ultimately alienating them within the relationship. He calls her back, panting, growling—

"When do you talk to this guy?"

"It depends, sometimes for hours. Every day this week."

"On the phone?" Shawn is panicking.

"Usually we talk over computer, we write each other."

He rests his head on the cold toilet. A long blue tear repairs in a tomb of ethereal plush matter, and just as it is possessed, objectified by his pupils, incalculably soft, tough, as if pained with jagged dental strife, he clasps a tendon with his pincers: *my bunny, my muffin bum, my jaded eel, hissing in a tank.*

"Are you listening to me? I need to follow my heart. I don't want to be a voodoo doll for your self-desire," Crystal says. "Besides, you fucked Robin and didn't tell me. You probably fucked Chelsey, too."

"And *you're* a saint? You're like a hamster in a cage, crawling over your little brothers and sisters, humping people on the wheel."

Shawn has no voice, no pulse; he just watches himself: a lowly flicker of skin and eyes in the unlit bathroom. In his warmish glow, bits of earth around his earlobes and mouth, he barks into the phone, and as it disconnects, so does Shawn, who spills himself into the empty bathtub. He wears her tattoo in the tub: *I want to see other people. You are so immature.*

3.

Oh, you would have laughed to see how cunningly they thrust me in here! Into the dirt. But you did see it, you must admit you saw it happen. I moved so slowly, very, very slowly, through the air, and after, so they assumed me dead, just like Perry all those years ago in the book of crap.

It takes me an hour to wriggle my whole head out of the edge of the windowpane, only to tumble back down, look to my left, and see miniature Shawn, Crystal, and Jim in their various tunnels and bedrooms, living and vacuuming, consuming themselves. He looks calm, Shawn does, as he lies upon his bed. Ha! Would a madman have been so sweaty and honest as this young punk, young dire poet, dying and drying up, in his homemade DIY embalming kit, legs and back in knots?

I'm fully collapsed; rain is now my only visual theatre, dirt the only scent or feeling. My head is swelling and

my view from here is shrinking, swallowed in dispropor-
tionate black. I hear a car fading north. The earth envel-
ops and holds me. The earth is disgusted with me. The
car fumes are frail and distant. I open my vermin eyes,
lightly dammed with fistfuls of city soil, maybe fingernail
scratches. Forest soil. A windowpane has been jammed
into the open mouth of my personal dirt hotel room. This
hole that holds me. Crystal and her friends and lovers are
long gone. It's God and me.

I'm more certain than ever. My hangnails are crimson
and fresh, my knotted stomach is loosening. My elbow
pushes my sweater into the pocket of earth. The feeling of
restriction is instant, comforting. I'm a chipped porcelain
rip-off, a paper plate, the best ever. I'm not epic but em-
balmed from sensation; tingle, tingle little star. I wipe the
tears from the side of my face. I can see through the window; the rain has slowed down to a wet blur and the sky
is turbulent with prehistoric stars. Tiny white pills feeling
the night: dissolving into one, into me.

I sleep inside of death's little rehearsal, and as I sleep,
that predawn moment fireworks its hot snuff down on me,
and Shawn's morning bedroom is full of beautiful prowl-
ers in their corduroy indecisiveness. And, yes, he's still a
little worm.

When she touches him he feels his confidence-balloon
shrink; Shawn can visualise his entirety: each synapse, ar-

tery, and minute cartilage recoils and denies its real estate as if the self-portrait is dismembering itself.

"You all right, Chels?"

Rain jewels on the early evening shingles. His phone is unplugged and her comfortable body forgives him: Chelsey puts a soft cheek on his rough neck and they lie together in a heap of teenaged rubble—boxes, things ready to move out, his bedroom rug rolled up—listening to Oldies. So quaint she thinks, and her body forgives him, the early evening rain jewelled, and the forgiveness like a terrible rebirth—her mind: never. Playing on Chelsey's susceptibility, the immediacy he felt in her nervous lust when she returned from the washroom down the hall, his parent's house and all, them being out, and her saying, "I want to stay," and Shawn not so sure, "I could be in a lot of trouble here, Chels, they want me out," and "I'm really trying to have sex," she says, her tiny rose lips looking both ways before crossing his borders—"and I'm still attracted to you, Shawn," and the little worm Shawn pulls her toward his chest. Like a werewolf, like Dracula, like a worm in a cape with hair all over its skin; he is one big knife blade humming so loudly no one can hear it, the same way the earth spins so fast. (At least that's what he believes from trying to study science.) So fast, we can't feel it.

It's been nearly two months since he's kissed her—a distortion washes over Shawn's greyscale peripherals: so many gestures, numbers, scents, and body types had comforted him—two months since she had gone back with Allen, only to run back, a look of shock on her face, a strange, wilting regret; and then, as they had so many times before work, quick like a bunny. So many gestures, numbers, and scents—tags, noses nuzzling, and naked breasts against his chest, fingers caressing him—the return of Chelsey comes out of nowhere. Even Robin saying, "Crystal's her arch-enemy, what were you thinking?" He is now hunting, willingly hunting in a game that will never end—the natural, easy, instinctual attraction game: where each person uses his or her unspoken love muscles to pull and tear like a stipend, or range of currency.

"Are you sure?" Shawn asks.

They have sex: a bit rusty considering it's been two months, and the circumstances—barely midnight on a Saturday with zero build-up. Shawn will later text her: "zzeerrrooo build up, then what? Flood gates? Confus-a-looozled, Chels."

The coke is still charging through him and all electrical, twitching in half-sleep, half-skeleton state. He feels its dead white drip down the back of his nose, down his throat, like he's swallowing a skinned ghost or something scarier. He hears a car horn. He hears a doorbell. It's his home and Chelsey is passed out on his chest.

In the early afternoon she leans against his burgundy

curtains, stroking them in a navel-gazing pose—familiarizing herself with the cut as if it were him, their first time, his sleeve.

"You want something to eat, Chels?"

Cooking for her calms the worm—spaghetti, green beans, carrot sticks, tomato soup, and toast. "I like it when you crunch." Spicy even, cumin, soup, and toast. "I like it when you crunch," Shawn says.

A minute . . . half an hour . . . two DVDs later . . . late afternoon . . . make out . . . it's nearly supper when her mother comes.

"There'll be enough parties in your future, Chelsey!" her mother says, picking her up from Shawn's place. "You don't have to go out so late."

"It's not even a school night," Chelsey protests, eyes still on Shawn at the door. Closing the door.

"Just some friends, Mom," Chelsey goes.

Mom huffs and drags Chelsey to the dark where the car is parked.

4.

Can I please mention once more from here, since there is not much room: it is not the young man Shawn who vexes me, but his wormy, gooey centre, the way I can see the folds of his dirt-covered stomach straighten and ooze, flatten and bulge. And every morning now, his blond-orange wavy hair, all starch and no life, haunts me, his light eyes as well, wolf-like. I will feel him in my desert teeth when the day breaks its incubator yoke, and I will boldly walk from my chamber-pot bedroom coffin and speak courageously to him, asking him why he would dare to jump through my sprinkler, which he did not ask to turn on, and dance his little dance of death, with me calling him by name in a apoplectic tone: "Shawn Michaels, you little piece of shit! Why are you here with a steak knife between your teeth? Why are you and Jim and Crystal and Robin, too? Why are you so ruthless in your macabre devotion to seamless night?" And here I am, digesting bits of his skull, but he's still alive and all, and I'm inquiring how he has passed the night. He dies and lives inside me intestinally, so you see he would have to be a very quick-to-the-point, not-drag-it-out kind of teen. Indeed, to suspect that every night, just at twelve, I look in upon him while he sleeps.

More announcements peter through the rain drizzle streams, through the tiny crack in the windowpane that I stare up at from my happy grave of life: *Maudlin Animal Services is working closely with Maudlin Police, the Ministry of Natural Resources, and Maudlin Parks and Recreation to locate and destroy the animal. There have been no incidents of rabies in coyotes reported in Maudlin in recent years; however, as a precaution, the animal will be tested. Residents are advised to avoid G. Ross Lord Park near Locust and Finch and Earl Bales Park near Sheppard and Bathurst if at all possible. Residents who must enter the park should take the following steps to protect themselves*:

- Do not approach the coyote.
- Do not go into the park alone.
- Do not leave children unattended.
- Keep dogs on leashes at all times.
- Remain on clearly marked paths and in busy areas; all the bites have occurred in less-travelled areas of the parks.
- Residents who encounter a coyote should not run

away. Stand still and make noise, e.g., yell, clap your hands. This will help scare the coyote away.

• Anyone who sees a coyote should call Maudlin Animal Services immediately.

Before passing out, I paint a dream template of myself replacing the bulbs the children ate from my front lawn after steak-knife dancing so cleverly, so cunningly, that no human eye—not even mine—could have detected anything wrong, so that my uncle's house, my dead uncle's house, the one I write in, so that its garden will never die. The weeds are witnesses to this clever tightrope-walking dream.

The night is well done, open wide, wide open, and grows frantic as I gaze up night's simple skirt with perfect distinctness—a dull dark blue with a hideous veil over it that chills my very marrow, a veil of pinprick stars the colour of marrow. Who has time to know? How can I research properly, confined to this tomb? Coming to my ears is a low, dull, quick sound, like a robotic insect or television microphones enveloped in cotton and lowered into an insect's larval state for a news clip. I know this sound well, too well. It is beating like a heart, its fury increasing. It's like a drum machine. The sound freaks me out.

5.

Look at me! I'm disgusting-looking! I look like shit! All covered in twigs, branches, and city sewer soil, a kind of caked gunk-slime, darker than outer space, runny, and just—I mean, suppose you're talking to somebody, let's say a woman, who's in a difficult mood, you just, you know, you try and calm her down but then her gang of fuckheads who are all—Forgive my jaded-eel-hell-hound-rabies-scabies outlook, but they're all like, "Crystal, we'll do anything for you, we'll throw this guy into a hole" (with tiny worm teenagers clinging to roots along the wet sides), "shall we toss this guy in this fucking hole, or what say you?" Last night in my stupor I said such awful things and had such awful thoughts.

You've got to be joking me. A little teenager in the ground, buried like a piece of fat in a cross-section of my mother's toxicology meatloaf? Relatively few people realize that the common earthworm, of which the best known species, but not always the most common, is called *Lumbricus terrestris* by biologists, are just as much new-comers to North America as we are. In fact, there are many areas in Canada where earthworms are absent and where the productivity of the soil could be substantially increased if they were introduced.

Earthworms are most numerous in grasslands and mull soils, relatively rare in acidic soils, and intermediate and variable in numbers in arable lands. However, other factors such as soil texture, moisture, temperature, and food supply also determine whether a field may have more earthworms than one on a neighbouring farm.

Were there others in the park? Watching me getting tossed around like a dead Christmas tree? Perhaps walking their dog? Always someone watching . . . I am awoken in my park coffin condo by a milk truck veering on some wet cement. The park is surrounded by a long, winding road.

Last night, before seeping into the abject earth of Maudlin's crust, before the angry farm hands tried to delete me from my own hard drive, I may have leaned my eyes through the beads of raindrops. Since this constellation is easily viewable as two parallel stick figures, I could have spent time strengthening a will to leave. If I had stared at the faintest contours of Castor and Pollux, collectively known as the Dioscuri, I may have tried to think of strange new beginnings, two halves, and the myth of these twins and their heavy concerns of cattle theft. In my semi-concussed sleep I may have been visited by the glimpsing Milky Way, or nuzzled by a herd of grateful dairy that I had set free with my thick mulch-gravy thoughts.

I pull myself out now, take three deep breaths, and begin my walk home from the park where that date ended so badly. Even as I write this true fact down on the smallest piece of paper imaginable, the muscles in my wrists feel altered. I can see the service station in the distance as I quicken my pace, scribbling, "ankle welts and aspirin ground into my temples; my forehead is missing."

I am writing up and down in the mud and of the heart. OF THE—a popular linguistic construct, has never been more simply presumed, prescribed, and essentially daft: I climb out of the hole that that bitch and her pump squad tossed me into. I shiver from the frozen lakeside nether-grave, walk down the street, up the street, back into Maudlin City's core.

Oh, you see, I am love's fledgling customer, on the verge of losing everything, who had almost lost it all. I could have died in that hole. It was just how I dreamt it would be a decade ago with Perry. A whole chapter was dedicated to the windowpane imagery, the grave, etc.—how highly choreographic and precise, even mapped out, to find a way of transporting me/Perry to the site. And as I lay there in my/Perry's own sorrow and loneliness, no longer required for a pedestrian work rate or duty of any kind, I thought: *This is not why people write books.*

I, Charles Haas, cannot be killed by characters, or those assumed to be characters. Those characters who read my old drafts, somehow fumble upon them in basement boxes, and re-enact an abject morality play, those who find my old manuscript pages in their kitty litter, cast the story, and star me in the ground—No! You would have to graft and feed me daily, exposing my legs and guts to Maudlin's finest frost if you wanted to rub me out. When I was lying in the ditch (nearly two hours have passed since I pulled myself out of the hole and moved the paint-chipped beauty of the plate glass window with my freezing, pruned digits), there was nothing I couldn't imagine:

And the final scenes of the mad, sweat-drenched dance party get all macabre and orchestrated by this orgiastic hood named Shawn. And he's rigged all these caskets, prop caskets, and roped all his hot young girlfriends into tending bar and coat check, and they use this defunct bar, right, and they get, like, two hundred people paying cover at the door, so they're doing okay, and they have booze and pills, and they're selling dimes and Ecstasy as well, right, and the party gets busted by the cops, and so, right, back to these prop coffins hanging from meat hooks. Shawn has spent, like, a real long time figuring out how to really fuck up the night, and there are real live teenagers inside each coffin.

Each coffin is rigged with a camera and they've fish-hooked these small microphones too, and so Shawn begins telling the kids in the coffins that he's lined them with needles full of poisonous drugs, or he's gonna cut off their oxygen—one of the two, I haven't decided. Meanwhile the cameras are all hooked up to his computer and he's projecting their inner realities on a screen with this live feed commotion, and wires are everywhere, and everyone is wired and paranoid because maybe the club is not licensed or some coincidental infraction occurs—the cops show up and the music is super loud so no one can hear the screaming. And if they do end up turning off the music, and the screams can finally be heard from within the coffins, they'll say it's just the video. And for a moment the cops will look at one another and say, "Well can you turn it down?" And that's when Shawn will talk into his microphone that goes into the coffins and say something creepy like, "If you say anything, I'll inject you on the spot and you'll fucking die. Just shut up." Something really psychotic.

Still, I haven't thought of a true ending. In many ways, those kids are still dancing and the drugs will never end and they'll just sort of implode through brutal endorphin-ecstasy-cocaine-semen-bleach-shit overkill, a sick blending of teenaged liquids that Shawn was going to cook up and inject his victims with. Then I thought his love interest would have an older brother or romantic rival and he'd overhear Shawn's plan and outsmart him, maybe take the coffins off the meat hooks even before the cops come, right, and load them onto a pickup truck and be like: "Shawn, you and your psycho friends have one hour to come up with two grand, or I'm driving to the bridge just off Weston Road, and I'm tossing your four coffin-nated pals into the river. Your prints are all over the coffins, inside and out. You're totally fucked. I also have print outs of your email plans from my sister's computer."

6.

Prop Casket $45.00

- Not for final disposal use
- Assembly is fast and simple with no tools required
- Environmentally friendly, produces no pollutants
- Can be shipped anywhere, 6' long
- Black with red interior

WRONG BAR BY CHARLES HAAS
fourth draft January 200–

I switch formatting here so watch out. Sometimes it's just straight-on sex, sometimes there is actual writing. I like switching the formatting—like sometimes it's a novel, then a play, then a paper airplane, then you're taking the pages and cutting them across my face, writing me a note. Okay Cate, I'm just joking. So this is like the pre-coffin-party build up. I have a few versions of how I think it should go—

The first scene is Shawn Michaels and Robin Beedie waiting outside a restaurant, maybe smoking or something. The restaurant is small. Shawn is going off on some tawdry tangent, all alchemy and the undead.

EXT. STREET—NIGHT

"I've watched it," Shawn goes.

Robin shrugs.

"I've seen it twitch." Shawn is a total worm tonight, sweating like foreskin in August. It's mid-autumn and everything is drizzly grey.

"What*ever* are you talking about?" Robin asks. They are standing on the corner. It's the middle of the night and Robin is shivering.

"Seen what? Well?" Robin is now interested in Shawn's confession because he has stopped speaking to her altogether and is dramatically running his hands through his hair: "I'm so greasy."

"Gross," Robin goes. "So . . . *You've seen* . . ." Robin wants to know now. She checks her watch. Crystal is supposed to be coming for dinner too.

"Watched it lie there, still, all forever-like." Shawn looks all over the road.

"What!?" Robin screams, laughing, so tired, she is so very tired. "What are you talking about?"

"I know death. At work with my uncle one time, before he died. My uncle. Every Saturday, Sunday, and Monday. Ate my lunches beside it. Two summers," Shawn says, taking her hand in his. "Munch, munch by the corpses."

"Stop it, you're getting creepy."

"Call the cops then. You runaway." Shawn points to the silent cars, the cat, the eaves. "All this," he motions, "this is . . . it's false. This here, in the dark, the music. The dead keep away from all this."

Jim and Crystal walk toward them from both (east and west) sides, grinning and bearing secret wounds.

"I worked at a funeral parlour for two summers. Nothing but chemicals and sonnets."

INT. JIM HELWIG'S LIVING ROOM—EARLIER THAT NIGHT

The formatting here is really cool, something happened in the edit, like when Radiohead played back "Creep" and it had that cool feedback guitar blast that was a total fluke. Well this edit is like that with the characters names in capitals and it's all smooshed like they're being thumbscrewed . . . I should go—

CLOSE-UP on Crystal Rowles's behind. Jim Helwig's hand lifts up her skirt and bends her over. Her hands clasp the coffee table in front of the couch. He pulls her tights down, revealing a panty-less behind. He gently spreads her lips with his forefingers, licks his other hand and sticks two fingers inside. CRYSTAL (Fixing her hair in the big living room mirror) We're going to be late. JIM I *need* to fuck you. (He's breathing heavily now, getting excited. He licks his thumb, spreads her cheeks and gently eases it into her ass.) CRYSTAL Oh God. (She doesn't have to say "FUCK ME," but thinks it. Jim fucks Crystal hard from behind, she clenches her face in a familiar clamp; he can see it in the living room's large mirror.) JIM Look at me Crystal, look at us. CRYSTAL Oh God, fuck! Yes! JIM (Licking his fingers like a disgusting animal) Take it, you take it. CRYSTAL God, it's so good . . .

V/O *So more or less they fuck and chew gum and rush to meet Shawn and Robin six blocks west. You can't just put them in the ground where you want the worms to break down a lot of waste. They each have their own muted and fluorescent desires and landscapes, their own vernacular, colour scheme, and blushing patterns. There are many other options for worm farms, from raised old baths and wooden box structures to covered rows on the ground. I feed them nothing but the earth they conquer and caress. They sleep on steak knives.*

INT. WHITE ORCHID RESTAURANT—NIGHT

A middle-class restaurant infused with gold chiffon and red velvet in East Maudlin. The decor is a mixture of faux-Oriental New Year's and mermaid subordination, with milky coral lime curtains, ransom text menus, and lemon eel-pattern tablecloths decorated with arrangements of twigs and seashells, encroaching white orchids stuffed crudely in large snail shells. Earlier this year, the decor was a mixture of 1990s faux-goth and hippie cottage, with velour curtains, homemade paper menus with burned fringes, and pale yellow tablecloths that would have been an eyesore if it wasn't for the low-watt lighting the restaurant insisted upon. Now everything's a bit more flare-gun obvious. Soon, night will conquer: drinking, dancing, denim, a ruckus of nicotine spit, police-hating crowds of people in the taboo dance club district. Gawkers. Dancing as the new child pornography—It's a Thursday in October.

SHAWN Strange decor, Helwig, you come here a lot? JIM Yeah, with you, last month for Robin's birthday. SHAWN Right.

The clientele is young, poorly dressed in the height of early-twentieth-century style: pouting girls in froppy jumper dresses, miffy eyes reflected poorly in tequila bottles with fluorescent worms swimming lively; aqua blue leggings and big white T-shirts; or tube tops and jean skirts; guys in ill-fitting power suits, or white blazers with jeans and T-shirts.

CLOSE-UP on a waiter bringing another basket of bread to the small table and looking oh-so-put-out and unimpressed. SHAWN (Mumbling) Probably a lousy actor. WAITER We have an appetizer special tonight, sweet potato fries and green beans with perogies. For entrees tonight there's a roast beef platter. SHAWN We're waiting on some friends, water for now, maybe a glass of wine? WAITER I'll need ID. JIM Busted. I'm good—wine for me. I'll drink it in front of him. Turned legal on the weekend. SHAWN You would do that too, on top of everything else you put me through. Putz. JIM Putz? No one says that anymore. SHAWN Who cares what *no one* says, dickwad. JIM There are the girls. Over there. (He points to a pair of gangly twenty-year-old girls in miniskirts and frilly blouses; both have dark slicked-back hair and horn-rimmed glasses and look all coquettish. Jim sniggers to Shawn something to the effect of: It's another campy night.)

INT. WHITE ORCHID—DINING AREA

Robin Beedie, Crystal Rowles, Jim Helwig, and Shawn Michaels are seated at a table set for five. The girls are quasi-dating both Jim and Shawn somehow, in some way. Lee Showles, the dishwasher at both White Orchid and Frisk Nightclub, just took three giant trays into the kitchen.

CLOSE-UP on various diners as we hear fragments of JIM and SHAWN Are you even capable of getting an erection? Where are you going to get the ID for tonight, dude? You're screwed. ROBIN (Staring at two waitresses) Do you think any of these guys will serve us? JIM Probably not. SHAWN Jim is being a real prick. Let's just get someone to buy us booze down the street, it'll take a few minutes. Just sweet talk them, one of you two. CRYSTAL You wish. We're going to Frisk tonight, right? SHAWN Yes, in like an hour. That's what we're doing, spotting the club to see if it's a good place for our night. You gotta get a look at the deejay booth and all that crap, drink prices, the look of everyone. ROBIN We'll get in, I know the guy. He works here too. JIM You get Kim to come? SHAWN Yeah. You talk to her about the night, next week? We need all the girls in there. WAITER And would you like a drink? ROBIN Vodka soda. WAITER No problem. Miss? CRYSTAL Same. CLOSE-UP on Shawn's jaw dropping. JIM We switched waiters, you should have ordered something, idiot. SHAWN (Listening to Crystal sniffing) How's your cold? CRYSTAL S'okay. S'all right.

There's a harsh circus of sounds: in Shawn's mind porcelain plates containing endangered meals crawl still life on the plate, eel-glistening desserts wobble on their small plates. The camera moves in on Shawn as his narration begins: SHAWN (V/O) *We're killing time stabbing ourselves in boredom, sitting in White Orchid, this crummy restaurant in the Greek district in East Maudlin.* The waitress winks at the young men at another table across from Shawn, and his face registers his convincing disgust. She sets down plates of fries and steaks and salads; a deluge of heavy eating will ensue, this also disgusts Shawn. As the waitress flirts with the adjacent men, we hear Shawn's description of each of his friends at the table: SHAWN (V/O) *You'll notice Robin, the little spider-egg hatchling, always has a goofy, glue-sniffed look on her face, while Crystal seems to always hold her jaw in some strange lock, as if she's swallowed a large cartoon key. Jim is nearly always sweating, his short Nazi haircut beading with sweat under the harsh lights here in glorious White Orchid.*

ROBIN God, I hate this place. This is a dead person's restaurant. For retards. It's so old, everyone here is, like, a hundred. I'm a young girl. SHAWN Okay, calm down, just don't start choking on bread. Let's go get something to hold us over for the next few hours. Asshole, any ideas? JIM Asshole? Is that any way to talk to me? SHAWN Why, 'cause you have a fucking fake ID I'm supposed to treat you like the Governor General? CRYSTAL Why aren't we at my place? I have stuff there. The group looks at one another.

EXT. STREET OUTSIDE WHITE ORCHID—NIGHT 10:15 P.M.

Chelsey Eaton locks up her bike. She leaves a book in Robin Beedie's bicycle basket with a note: "In a rush. Later. Love, Chels." After securing the book and letter, she realizes she must use the washroom.

INT. WHITE ORCHID—WASHROOMS

SHAWN (Coming from the Men's) Hey Chelsey, what are you doing here? CHELSEY Just dropping a book off for Robin, one I borrowed. You? SHAWN Here with Robin and Crystal and Jim, too, we're going to check out Frisk later. CHELSEY I gotta go. I'll talk to you later. SHAWN Chels. CHELSEY I can't get into this, I can't. You're pathetic. JIM (He burps, approaches Shawn) Who's that? SHAWN (Throws a dirty look at him, bordering on partial fellatio) Fuck off, Jim, just go back to the table will you? (Lee Showles enters from the back of the kitchen, he's tall, greasy black hair, well-worked arms, long face, knows Robin and Crystal and Chelsey) LEE (Carrying dishes) Hey girl. CHESLEY Hi, how are you? LEE Good. You look lovely.

INT. WHITE ORCHID—DINING AREA—EVENING
(Draft two)

CLOSE-UP on porcelain plates containing hummus, a cornucopia of raw vegetables, and a smattering of shapely crackers descending onto two tables. It's a popular appetizer. Crystal Rowles, Robin Beedie, Shawn Michaels, and Jim Helwig are at a table set for four. The girls are wearing short dresses and theatrical silk gloves, while the boys are in jeans and casual dress shirts—lumberjack plaid.

The camera moves in on Shawn as his narration begins: SHAWN (V/O) *The dinner is being paid for by all the advance tickets I've sold to my wonderful dance party. I've presold a thousand tickets, with another forty coming in late tonight via PayPal. We're sitting in White Orchid, Nouvelle Vague is playing on the stereo, and the girls are loving every second of it. I could say that the party will be great and this whole scene here, this street, will become the new hot spot but I wouldn't know what I was talking about. Frisk is the name of the club we're going to, by the way, if you get lost from the ransom letter text menus or the washroom—is that Chelsey?* The Waiter pours the girls some red wine. As he does so we hear Shawn's description of each of the people at the table: SHAWN (V/O) *I love dirt: You'll notice that my friend and I, and to some extent the girls, all have ghastly pale features. Our skin is light, and we all have dark hair (except for me), dark eyes (for the most part), and a certain college-level bravado. Jim's hair is usually blond, but he's been shaving his head lately, maybe he's going through some sort of insect phase; he's been wearing a lot of insect-print T-shirts lately. The warmth of the restaurant is making him perspire more than usual. Although I've been urging him to wear suit jackets on these nights, he's settled for a simple green golf shirt with a thousand ants all over it. Very campy. Helwig is the biggest asshole sometimes; his promo-tional theories are convoluted and warped, wrapped up in a micromanaging varnish that makes me gag. He can go on and on sometimes; I'm sure he'll become a big CEO some-day. I always snap his training bra. Robin Beedie is the yes girl. Crystal, or Crystal Balls (actual last name is Porcupine, I think—no, Rowles, actually, she just corrected me), is the unpredictable one you really have to wonder about—that is, how soon before she's owned by the mafia? Robin keeps sig-nalling me in a very obvious way, even though I've invited no such communication and haven't suggested the slightest desire to talk in body code. It's about 10:43 now, the food seems to be taking forever.*

SHAWN (Flapping his napkin across his chest and face) So I want to talk for a moment, change the subject and talk, um, about these robot wasps, okay? There is this term for them; hold on, I think I wrote it down on this business card because I wanted to research it for a possible Halloween costume. CRYSTAL A possible torture device then, eh? SHAWN You wish, Crystal, you wish. No, a brain-boring robot that burrows its way through tissue in the same way a wasp digs through wood could make keyhole surgery safer. To bore into wood, the wasp rapidly oscillates backwards and forwards. CRYSTAL Oscillates *wildly*? SHAWN Yes, just like the Smiths song. Its sharp teeth catch in the wood and prevent the wasp from retreating, it can insinuate itself into the wood with the minimum amount of force. A team of mad scientists, well, they're mimicking this mechanism to create a medical probe. JIM That's great, Shawn, maybe you can get a transplant. SHAWN You really think that would help you out, don't you, Jim? Replacing me, huh? JIM I don't understand. SHAWN You don't? You understand all this that's happening, the here and the now, the things you get to do in your life now, because of me, right? You feel those things, you understand that feeling, right? JIM I can't feel what my eyes don't see, Shawn. SHAWN Then you don't feel much, do you Jim?

7.

I'm halfway home.

I'm thinking, but about nothing much past the meat-hook part. It's quite cold outside. They put the coffins on the meat hooks, something bad happens. Fuck, I'm dirty, covered in night's natural vomit. As I said, you know, somewhere, if you take all the people dancing in a line and add them to a narcissistic nympho soup, they'll eventually become bone, just melt and explode their batteries.

Morning still . . .

I pass two gas stations and three hotels. I approach the only stretch in Maudlin that comforts me. I hear two girls smoking outside. How can I hear girls smoking? Okay, so I assume they're smoking because it feels like it is minus 450 and no one else is on the street and they are pacing and shivering outside a bar. The bar is open. I plan on going straight inside when I hear one of the girls talking about masturbation, so I stop to tie my shoe. One has a fake fur coat, the other a marshmallowy white winter jacket.

"I forced water into my, you know, for well, yeah, m-m-masturbation and well . . ."

"Well? You drown your snatch?"

"Naw."

"It felt good?"

"It depends on how much pressure and how high the water was forced in."

"I use those water jets in the pool to get a thrill, but I let the jet hit my bikini bottoms so it doesn't actually go up . . . you-know-where. It feels awesome."

My shoes are now tied. I look down at the cuffs of my tan pants, mostly black from oil or coal, charcoal. Somehow Shawn and Crystal managed to find a park close to the lake; I suspect the plan was to drown me or take me sailing, then dump me in the middle of the lake like an aging relative, an oversized goldfish. Well I showed them . . .

Finally rerouting myself to a more reasonable location, i.e., home, I enter my house, feeling like a stale, unsalted cracker. I have two hours to submit a grant report for Maudlin City's Writers Well program, or else they'll come and flood my apartment. It has to be three thousand words long and incorporate how my daily life has been issued a subpoena into bliss and lucidity as a result of the four hundred dollars the council has vacuumed from their waiting room/interrogation chamber couches and stuffed into an envelope for me. I decided to write about—

I look outside and see young people kinking hoses on the lawns around me. They're like tiny arteries and veins and circuitry in the city.

I set my keys down on the dining room table and discover a series of communications: irregular fax and voice message beeps weakly flash red in the diminutive daylight, somehow gasping for recognition on the jagged remains of my answering machine, while in the mailbox, there is a large silver letter.

"What in God's concrete whirlpool is this?" I declare, opening it at the sink where I'm waiting for the water to get cold. The letterhead has the most insane logo I've ever seen: an aggressive blender with red laser eyes. Aggressive blender red laser eye logo is trademark of K.L.O.S.U.R.E. GROUP 200–.

K.L.O.S.U.R.E. 6.0 is on its way to you. It will be installed in four days. You have twenty-three hours to accept these terms. The terms are being sent to your current address. Your current address is 73 Oakwood Crescent. To confirm your address please call 542-252-2999. Confirmation No. A900M735556FHM. Instructional material will follow. You will not be billed for this service. Materials will be shipped within 24 hours of acceptance of terms.

Curious and paranoid is not a law firm but my convincing state. I have also just discovered a handwritten note from Cate stuck to the fridge: "Came by to pick up my address book, which I left in the washroom. When I was here someone robotic called about a K.L.O.S.U.R.E. thingie. I think there's a letter too, about the same thing. There were faxes too. Good luck, Chucky! C.A.T.E."

I call the number on the K.L.O.S.U.R.E. letter and pound in my confirmation number: "PRESS 9 IF YOU ACCEPT, 7 IF YOU DO NOT. IF YOU WANT MORE INFORMATION PLEASE PRESS O TO SPEAK WITH A K.L.O.S.U.R.E. REPRESENTATIVE."

Pressing 9, I sit down on the couch and turn on the television to see if I am on the news. My sense of purpose is now endangered. After hours of deleted scenes, after turning over, kicking out sheets, drinking three glasses of water, tasting culinary odours from meals I do not feel responsible for nor remember curating—it is a cold morning. After dressing and combing, I am ready to leave the house, a few more bites of toast, a few sips of tea—A KNOCK ON THE DOOR!

"Well there goes my life!" I say, each step numb, full of pep and cyanide. I'm due at the boardwalk in forty minutes.

I open the front door with gusto. "Hello?"

"Good morning, sir, glad I caught you," the peppy courier says. "Are you Mr Haas?" She's squeaky.

I say nothing.

"Sir?"

Okay, Jesus, I'll talk, I say to myself.

"Yes," I go. The courier passes me the letter, again silver. "Where did this come from?"

The courier shakes her head. "I'm not sure, sir, let's have a look." She takes it back from me and flips it over, then back again normal-ways.

"No return address?" I ask with a desired level of confirmation expected from my tonal output. "Well?"

"Says here in tiny it's a PO box in Leatherpalm. That's about six hours north of here. Big spice city."

"I see."

The courier is holding out a pen. "Sign?"

"Sure." I sign. The envelope is fonted with the following declaration: "K.L.O.S.U.R.E. is coming! Read me! Believe me!"

I now know that any union to which I am equated could not sustain life or an emotional structure, and this (or any future) package is and will be evidence, bordering on forensic. Cate's departure is now for her own good more than anything else. Her reduced schedule a lifesaving device.

I type a single line on my rigor mortis typewriter, typos and all:

Who knews what the hell is on its way to destry me.

I've been reading about the scientists again, how they want to mimic wood wasps so they can do brain surgery. The scientists like the way they eat wood, these wasps. I try to get Cate interested, but she's in a rut: I suspect about Daniel.

"A wood wasp, also called a horntail, is in the family *Siricidae*. Females lay eggs in the bark of pine trees, using a needle-like ovipositor. This partnership between tree and wasp can cause severe damage to pine forests," I go.

"And now they're being put in people's brains?"

"No, they're just thinking about it."

"Thinking about putting wasps in people's brains?"

"They think the species' tunnelling methods are good enough to mimic with a robot—its methods, you see? Not real wasps; they would die inside your brain."

"They could colonize."

"You're missing the point. Cate, I can't work at that beach anymore; I mean, you work inside, you work from home, you have things, heat, life, lamps, clean socks. Outside, well, it's all about cruel realities as charter member of the Sisyphus Society for Sacked Lunches."

"Yeah. Drag," Cate goes. "I'm sorry, Charles, I'm really tired these days. Can't sleep."

"For about forty bucks you can buy a prop coffin made of cardboard or particle board that will add realism to your haunt."

"I see."

I feel like I'm in another dimension. I keep reading the text in front of me, all my fabulous print outs. *The coffin's dimensions: 74" x 22" x 12" inside—comes flat with an assembly time of approximately 30 minutes. Opt for Klasper-fasteners, which allow you to put it together and take it apart year after year, party time.*

"They suggest finishing the pieces before assembly." *Note: The basic model cannot be carried while occupied.* "You can add a thick bottom and you just got yourself a fully functional coffin that you can not only carry but bury as well."

"Okay, well, good luck."

"Cate!"

"Yeah?"

"The ideas are endless!"

"Talk to you tomorrow or something, Charles."

"I just love biomimetic robots, don't you?"

On Wed Sept 17, 200– at 12:28 AM, shawn g michaels <smichaels87@gmail.com> wrote:

dirty fun sexy lust dungeon rumour podcasts: 30 each, let's do like 4 or something or 1 min each. real hot and gossipy with voice overs, etc . . .

Dear JIM i know who you are.
how are you?
We got 3 coffins for the 29th! I mean 30th!
October!

i feel like satan!

love shawn

On Sept 17, 200– at 12:33 AM, jim helwig <Jimbgo2helwig@aol.com> wrote:

Dude, stop being insecure and call me or come over here and pick me up!

Jim

On Sept 17, 200– at 12:38 AM, shawn g michaels <smichaels87@gmail.com> wrote:

Okay, Ferris Bueller.

S.

8.

She said no way to going to Shawn's party. Chelsey is at home, studying and drinking hot chocolate. Crystal is stepping inside a coffin, as are Robin and Kimberly. Jim is helping them, and Shawn is taking money at the door. The night is extra windy and newspapers, fresh ones and old, scuttle about the entranceway like polluted bats.

"Lots of pussy cats, Shawn," Robin goes, pointing out a half dozen girls done up in faux whiskers and cotton-ball tails.

"Those are bunnies," Shawn corrects her, absorbing the night and its bedevilled carnival of saucy poses and cell-phone flashbulbs harking down on retinas.

The night is wet, full of cunning and lemon-wedge kisses. Cute dolls rolled up like kittens in a paper towel commercial, that's what he sees when he looks at the girls laughing across the club, waiting, chattering. They wear a look that leaves little of their translucent nature to the imagination—a tilted private-school uniform with something a bit more relaxed and saucy.

Definitely a class war motif going on with this playful outing. Shawn can't help but stare. The sweet sweater dresses with above-the-knee socks are simple and clean—an attempt at preservation and poise. Even the boys here at Frisk get a bit clean, with white pants and mod cut jackets, perhaps hiding something dark underneath. It is, after all, a Halloween party.

The sound bites are barbed in delicious funereal voyeurism, almost sci-fi camp. "Is there a camera in the coffin?" "Is there one in yours?" The girls chatter back and forth, at least that's what Shawn thinks he's hearing—"You okay in there?" he might have just said in passing, hard to hear over the clatter of noise.

How did people get here so fast? The 22 Corwell bus route operates between Corwell Station in the area of Corwell Avenue and Calf Street East and Binger Loop, generally in a north-south direction. Frisk is on 738 Calf Street East. You get a transfer from the station because sometimes the bus detours.

Three coffins, three girls, no cameras inside. The standard size is seventy-eight inches long, but one can be built to your particular body specifications. At the last minute Jim and Shawn ditch the hidden-camera idea because of technical impossibilities. Jim beckons Shawn toward him during a rather loud deejay set. Jim's face is sweating. The beats are particularly loud. His expression is that of terror and excitement. He doesn't know what to do with his face, so he does everything.

"Someone says they're going to rob you tonight," Jim goes. "Rob us, I mean, Shawn."

Shawn shakes his head.

"We're going to call the cops, right?"

Shawn shakes his head like it's all part of the plan. "Who told you that?"

Chelsey turns on the television and runs a bath. She locks her front door. She puts her iPod on shuffle. She gets a thick towel from the hall closet and walks naked toward the bathroom. She puts shampoo in the bath and decides to wash her hair as well.

Inside her coffin, Crystal is bored and gets out. She goes in and out freely.

"Hi Shawn."

Shawn nods. Jim walks off. "Get Robin out, we're going for a smoke."

Robin and Crystal go outside for a cigarette and are nearly blown away it's so windy.

"Jesus, girl, we're going to blow away."

Lee joins them outside for a cigarette. They giggle and

twirl in front of him.

Inside, the club smells like lip gloss and tongues. Jim mutters something to Shawn, who pretends he's listening to a cool story and doesn't show any signs of worry. Jim says to still watch out for the gate and appears nervous.

"You know, the gate where the money is taken and the tickets are dished out."

"I know what words mean, Jim."

Shawn carries all the money with him. The people at the door know this now and just hand him the money. Lee is bussing tables tonight and helping out. He is also whispering things to Shawn.

No more pre-sold ticket-holders in line. There is no more line; the club is nearly at capacity (280). People have told people there would be girls in coffins and it would be the best Halloween party in town. People are dancing, drinking, and merriment glows and jitters. Some prop coffin manufacturers have waiting lists. Shawn was lucky; he found three that fit his requirements in a warehouse online. Shawn doesn't feel lucky. He sees Steven Knight and knows him from before. From this one time he was talking with Lee. Lee comes behind Shawn and again whispers something in his ear.

AFTER A TEEN PARTY DANCE PRANK LED TO A SIXTEEN-YEAR-OLD GIRL'S HORRIFIC PROP COFFIN HILLSIDE DEATH, THE COMMUNITY WANTS TO AVENGE HER DEATH.

Last update: November 24, 200–, 9:05 PM

> this is so stressing, my dad heard this situation on the news and i'm 17 years old and he's so worried about me having an account every time i get an email . . . he's just checking on me to see who I'm chatting with but it doesn't bother me at all because i know he's doing it for my own safety.

Close comment
Register or log in to comment
1 comments | See all
Hide reader comments
Print this story

9.

"Cate? It's nearly Halloween. I know that thing is coming to get me. I have made serious errors and now my answering machine just sings in high pitch tones, belting out a most hazardous tune. This K.L.O.S.U.R.E. terror-rape-ro-bot-wasp thing is going to come get me, I just know it. You're likely out or screening your calls. I understand, I'd screen me too if I was on the other end, shotgun at the mouthpiece . . . voice over and out . . . Wait, anyway, I have been wondering what you are up to. How are you? Later . . . ah."

Who knows how many pieces of technology are right now recording my every meaningless, lonely movement? As I drip dry, I mumble into a towel's cotton infinity: "This would never happen if I lived by the sea . . . but it's happening to me. And, oh great, the red tide has short-circuited my poison ivy league heart, and the lacrosse team is aiming its collective stick right at the centre of my nose."

I pull out quickly from my substandard driveway and turn the radio on. I roll down the awkward windows. Each corner is another signal post, something in the distance keeping me framed in time-code reality. The air is cool and makes me feel like it's going to be a really great day. It could be a great day, a good day, yes.

And somehow I feel like my other body parts don't share this positive outlook. But I try to sidestep their brutality. Hell, I might even sneak a dip in the lake. Wait, hold on, I'm trying too hard to be normal and it hurts. My negative muscle couplings tighten in the mechanics of my lower quadrants. I can hear garbled language emitting from my seatbelt area in my own voice: "We're all really in quite a shock-shock." It's coming from an area north of my ankles, south of my belly button . . . no, my knee. Or knees? I can't tell.

I slam on the breaks, wishing my extremities would cease these riotous speeches. The sun is rising; the board-walk is illuminated, yellows and oranges dye the wood. I park the car and begin to haul my crap to the sand.

On the boardwalk my shift plays out in ninety swelled minutes of episodic sunstroke and migraines, broken up by two fifteen-minute breaks in the micro shade. The failure of my investigation here is matched by my crap sales.

By the time I get home all I can muster for dinner is a margarine lid of crackers and room temperature ginger ale, which I then proceed to throw up, pass it down to the carpet like a fungus lint ball bedaubed in my family's genetics on both sides; a fatal lint ball to be sure, mom and pop swab stop.

I feel a real fever, razor-real. One long pain pulse and one long dizzy spell. This is my moment.

Another package. I can't open it right away. I stare at the windowsill: three small cacti, a shoehorn, and a wine glass obstruct the waning sunset. I want all the light. Crawling on all fours, I paw the crackers pathetically, stare down at the package. The hobo tea spools around my face like a parasitic wraith.

"Oh sweet terror, I'm ripe for all the parties and all those concerned. It's party time."

A small gold envelope is glued to the silver box. The box is sealed in shrink wrap. I am thin-skinned and ready to boil over in tears. The wind begins to rattle the house. It makes a jarring sound along the eaves. I pull at the shrink wrap until I free the envelope. I open it: "Thank you for responding to our automated registration. K.L.O.S.U.R.E. has been ordered to visit you in the next ten days. To prepare you for this, we have enclosed some material to listen to, watch, read, and enjoy. Study carefully. Please be prepared for inevitable K.L.O.S.U.R.E. today!"

I open the box slowly, taking long breaks to poke my hobo herbal tea bag with a large spoon. I dim the lights and unplug the phone. The box has astonishing contents. It contains a booklet called MEET K.L.O.S.U.R.E. and brims with plastic-sealed electronic objects: a VHS tape, a DVD, a frayed wire battery or some sort of robotic crime scene organ donation, an antiquated CD-ROM, and something called an "audio cassette" chaotically labelled in red handwriting. Several glossy photographs and testimonials from satisfied users are also included. These glossies are disturbing, to say the least, which at this point is impossible. Some are suitable for framing.

I enjoy digging through the box immensely.

Near the bottom I find a pair of goggles, a can of WD-40, and a small flashlight. I put the VHS tape into the VCR and press Play. The tape begins to rewind.

"They can't even rewind their tapes? Nice company. Totally malevolent and cascading in depraved notions of labour-intensive anxiety. They must know their target users, or whatever I am supposed to be called. Not a client. Clearly someone has hired these people to destroy me. Big surprise. Didn't see that coming."

If I were the subject of a piece of fiction, at this point the narrator may begin to describe the whites of my eyes as "bleached in terror" as I watch the television screen, awaiting the signal to change from cable-out snow-static to signal 03 blue to Interpol piracy warning.

The frantic prose could continue in this neurotic pattern:

Here was a man, a bit of a man, with sacred tim-
ing and eerie pathos. He quaked at the quick,
jeering plastic jerk sound; the video digested in
the 2-head VCR and, stretching each strand of
tape across its retinal exaggerator, revealed to
Charles an even deeper reality, one that awaited
him in a matter of hours. This sense of pending chaos made Charles rock himself back and
forth maternally on the couch. Surrounded by
pamphlets and brochures that promised some
sort of justice, Charles began to panic.

Furthermore, one may write, "now visibly shaken, he
feels his stomach knot a noose as the video begins to play.
He would throw up the noose, ever a reminder of his options. He can taste his brain eating the sweat in his hair,
whether in forests, cities, parks, or condos, K.L.O.S.U.R.E. is
reality. The leader and principal shredder in any romantic
finality program, K.L.O.S.U.R.E. has no equal."

And so I tell the television, the empty house, I stand
up—"What about the cyanide-producing millipede,
Harpaphe haydeniana?"

No answer. Perhaps K.L.O.S.U.R.E.'s hearing isn't so hot.

The voice-over combs my sweat: *After extracting what
it needs from your once-loved one, K.L.O.S.U.R.E. releases a
local anesthetic, defecates a pellet of partially paralyzing,*

capsule-shaped used nutrients, which is covered with intes-
tinal mucus.

On the screen a large steel wasp (coated in translucent silver coating, a sort of armour, its wiry insides digesting a dozen long-stemmed roses and its mechanical mouth spewing small sparks) stomps around a small park, while its long multi-jointed legs pull its entire frame toward a man loading groceries into his car.

Twenty feet high if it's an inch. I feel sad. Retracting its wings and standing up on its back legs, the wasp reaches out for the man with its frontal limbs. It clasps him by the throat. As the man struggles, now suspended upside down from one leg, he screams. The robo-wasp lets out a set of high and low frequencies. It also begins stinging the man along his waist and stomach, slowly lifting up his dress shirt. I run my hands under the couch cushions, only to discover a can opener. Despair is all over me now in a wild rash.

The wasp is not done: just as the man gets to his feet, clutching his stomach, pawing the side of his car, the wasp lifts him up over the car, staring at him now with its giant-screen-television-sized head.

"Holy shit!" I go, watching the wasp toss the man like a cork onto the pavement. The voice-over chimes in with, *Digging a hole with its drill-bit stinger, K.L.O.S.U.R.E. 6.0 mock buries your ex in parking lots, or sometimes your ex's own front lawn for all to see! It all depends on what setting has been ordered. That's* K.L.O.S.U.R.E. *for you.*

I am seared in terror. Robot bugs mowing my lawn? Stealing my car and eating my groceries?

K.L.O.S.U.R.E. WORKS
Copyright 200–

A note is tied to the front porch.

Nice try. Not her handwriting at all. That agency is up to its usual paper-cut assault. Tampering and rewiring my reality. I begin to act terrifying.

"IT WON'T WORK! I'M NOT AFRAID OF K.L.O.S.U.R.E.! You fuckers will have to do better than this!"

A neighbour sitting in his backyard runs inside his house.

I gotta beef up security. I look at the sewer grate in front of the house as I drag the substandard lawnmower from the shed and flip the machine on, gunning it angrily. Dragging and steering, I perfect the chore until the tiniest uncut square patch of green grass remains. I gobble it up triumphantly.

I look down the road to my right: Nothing moving.

I look down the road to my left: Nothing moving.

It's not coming. "He's afraid," I go. "K.L.O.S.U.R.E., my ass," wrapping the extension cord up into my arms, bits of chewed grass clinging to my clothing. Night is coming.

Inside, I am nervous and pat a package of spaghetti as if it were a cat. I want to order a pizza but balk: what if the delivery person is mistaken for me? He gets attacked by a giant nuclear hornet and I'm charged with conspiracy to maim.

I'm starving.

I stretch out on my back lawn and quietly watch the families do their laundry and plan their lives. Some unload parcels, some pack up cars, some barbecue—they are professional. I read an old *National Geographic*. Night growls over Maudlin's harsh landscape: the once-calm beer-coloured sky is now a simple black felt backdrop with hints of underbelly lightness: it's manta-ray insane. The stumpy buildings are soft with pastel tones and rusty piping elaborately plotted around each angle, each dimple.

From inside now, I approach the mauve curtains and peer through a slit. The road is still. I watch the curb. The street lamp. I touch the curtain. "You've been a comfort, and mauve, this whole time. I've been alive up to now. My socks are soiled in who knows what. It's been a long day and I'm exhausted, curtains. What's next? What is going to happen?"

Just then I see the sewer grate slide open; slow and heavy is the big sound. Then, once the cover is off the cut sphere, a harsh, high-pitched electronic buzz is released, a giant, monstrous frequency.

"Mauve curtains, what was that? What's that buzzing noise accompanying this act of late-night bungalow terror?"

I am in the hallway. I am putting on my winter boots. From the hall closet I grab a tennis racket, toss it down, now I have a baseball bat.

A single siren, the pitch of grating fingernails along a cold chalkboard.

I open the front door. Now I'm standing on the front porch, flexing my muscles in pride not fear. I warm up the bat with swings. The sewer grate is glowing from its municipal pore. From within the hole a metallic limb clenching what appears to be a large pink dildo emerges.

I take off my shirt.

The limb pulls the body from the sewer grate hole. The torso, if you could call it that, is translucent and churns love letter fragments, photo booth pictures, and other miscellaneous artifacts. I know this because I studied the literature. Its head is silver and yellow, covered in sixty copper-coloured eyes pulsing rhythmically in a blue electronic outline. Parts of the torso are covered in mossy grey pubic hair and, upon recognizing me, at least I think that's what it's doing, its mouth begins to howl uncontrollably. Neighbouring houses light up. I pull a red plastic bucket from the bushes.

"Silica, meet K.L.O.S.U.R.E."

You wonder what I'm doing, neighbouring families, don't you? Well I'm putting on an undercoating in case this motherfucker tries to swallow me whole! I know you think I'm nuts, but if you saw the video, you'd know what this son of a bitch—oh man, my heart is racing. This thing is capable of some real cruel shit. You see, this stuff I'm putting on, this acts as a desiccant and strips the waxy coating off the cuticle of the insect, thus causing suffocation.

"So come and get it, honey!"

Its pinchers have me. And, yes, I'm already in tremendous pain. The machine's eyes concentrate on me, never relenting, never losing purpose. It hones in on me, and me alone.

Faintly, from the smallest speakers, a warbled love ballad leaks. I can almost make out the song. This is some great Halloween weekend—Oh Maudlin, take back this beast, back into your crusty asbestos bowels.

I pour the rest of the insecticide juice bucket over my head to protect myself, immediately feeling the sting. The creature draws near, raising itself nearly twenty feet above me before picking me up with a long limb: "We didn't use the word love a lot, did we?" I ask it.

The creature howls in return; its head turns to one side.

"When you love someone you say it, right there, out

loud. Otherwise the moment just—"

"Pazzzz yewww byyyyyyyyyyyyyeeee," K.L.O.S.U.R.E. says, finishing my thought exactly. I now know there is nothing I could say that the creature doesn't already expect me to say. Despite the night ahead of me, I feel a great sense of comfort, with all the confidence of a grade eight make-out king, daubed in just the right amount of cologne.

My face is scarred red in wet chemical tears; I quiver and spit and shake a foamy verbal confluence as I speak.

"Blahmala, I'm going to tell you, rafallalaraka, everything K.L.O.S.U.R.E. Get ready for fee fee fee foo, real horror, oh showayze . . . Get ready for love!"

Obsession

How I would like you, Night! without those stars
Whose light speaks a language I know!
For I seek emptiness, darkness, and nudity!
But the darkness is itself a canvas
Upon which live, springing from my eyes by thousands,
Beings with understanding looks, who have vanished.

—Charles Baudelaire

part four the death of the party

Come on, you have to laugh at the whole stupid, like, spectacle, the grim ritual of "I love this song" bullshit. Well, we'll print up tickets or something, anyway, while you keep up your grim appreciation of every stupid thugged-out hip-hop song on the market *and* the girls are having a cigarette. Let me tell you what we need to get in terms of organization. I mean, yeah, we have combative egos. I will work with you on it as a team, but right now we are developing it, and really NO ONE IS WATCHING US! So we have to get people paying attention. *We have to sell at least a hundred tickets in advance.* Don't worry, just realize I'm doing all the—hold on—Hey ladies, what's new? You want to rent movies or something? What? Talking about? Us? Human. Humanity. Humanity the musical. Just the party, the theme, you know. The club will be dark, right, so maybe we can get a black light, or body paint. What do you think? *Body paint might be fun, but messy.* Wait till you hear this idea, Jim, you'll think you've seen the world turned upside down. You'll see things my way, all poltergeists pole dancing. I'm tired of prom night's promise of real hot and gossipy madness. Frisk is perfect. *We just need a theme.* We have a theme. *What is it?* Can't say yet. I have ordered props though, and someone is helping to do the installing. You just get ready to help promote this, get people interested. *My sister is in my room, hold on. What? Get out! Sorry. Anyway, what?* Did you hear about that fire in Leatherpalm? *No.* Siko club. It went up in flames! *That new club?* Yes. All gone. And, like, thirty people were injured. Four died. *That's insane.* Yeah, over fifty people were treated for different things, and they thought at first, like, two hundred people were trampled to death, but then they started coming out, choking on smoke. *What started the fire?* They think it was a cigarette in the washroom. *Let's not have an inferno theme.* Noted. Say Jim, can you talk your friend Kimberly into working our night? *I could ask. What would she have to do?* Nothing, just hide in a box with Robin and Crystal. *What box?* I'll show you tomorrow. *My sister needs the phone.* Okay, well, I'll see you tomorrow in study hall then.

1.

Seventeen-year old's Lust Dungeon fantasy-turned-
tragedy has e-paper trail for the ages writes ▬▬▬▬

"I am waiting for a good movie to be made about me.
Who will play me?"—Shawn Michaels' message post in
June 200–, cribbed from an alleged Zodiac Killer letter
written in the early 1980s.

The Internet is the new high school hallway. For the 18-
24 demographic, which represents nearly 90 percent of
online social tech sites, the Internet is a must-have lifeline,
second only to the cellphone. Like high school locker chatter (there's still the hunk pin-ups) but with more sociable
visuals, sound bites and neon perma-glow profile stats
(relationship status vagaries are always on the dramatic
side), message boards, social sites, and personal pages cre-
ated for networking have started cropping up in concern

barometers of parents nationwide.

"The music blares when you click in, like you've accidentally bumped into a dorm room party blaze," Michelle Gagnon, 39, said when I asked her about her teenaged children's online activities. "You become the voyeur in the teenaged bedroom of your choice. It's easier than talking on the phone, quicker than walking over to your friend's place. It's a great go-between for those big moments like prom, parties, and going to the movies."

So if the Internet is filling in the deleted scenes of a normal teenager's life with constant human interactions, if someone is always watching, does that someone have to know the person they're watching? "Sometimes I guess you could be watched by people who you don't know," says Chelsey Eaton, an eighteen-year-old senior at St. Lawrence High School in Maudlin City.

In mid-September 200–, Chelsey received an e-greeting card with a small image of Bambi on it from her ex. It had been a few weeks since Shawn and Chelsey had stopped spending time together. "I fell for it," Chelsey told reporters, "and we semi got back together. But I felt so stupid. A part of me missed him a lot." Shawn's darker side was coming out in his missives and message board postings, which only seventeen people could read because of the way he had his settings.

END OF CLIPPING.

So it was more than money you think? I don't know (Both). *Did Shawn ever talk about Lee?* CR: Only in, like, typical jealous guy talk. RB: He always changed the subject so we rarely spoke of Lee in front of Shawn. *They must have had some sort of understanding?* Hard to say. It would be hard to imagine since they really didn't like each other. Jim might know, but his lawyers—(CR is tired and I'm asked to leave) RB: Where are Lee and Shawn? Like, why doesn't anyone know where they are?

2.

The night is a success of mulched cottons and majestic whimpers, each persona carrying its own secret weapon. Spongy lips, angel faces baptized in soft rain perspiration, egg-sized eyes batting playfully, while sex membranes glissade down the smalls of backs like medallions, touching down where target tattoos remain firm like bone itself.

The coffins hang obvious. People smack the sides and the girls' shrill voices inside draw jeers from the crowd. Jim and Shawn take turns telling people not to knock the stiffs.

"Don't mess with the dead," Jim goes. Shawn agrees, placing his arms across his chest.

Robin has to pee so she's helped down and out of her crypt. "It's stuffy in there," she says with a crooked pastel smile.

Bodies wobble against one another in a melee, like coral, like static in the dryer, animated and unforgiving bolts of energy. In short, this lust dungeon is a paradise, a simple, conquerable night of exuberance and charm. Simple. Simply that.

Two worms are joined by a mucus ring, they exchange sperm. The sound of the bass is hard. The mucus ring passes over the head of the worm as it hardens into a cocoon. The drinks are cold, mascara runs, throats become parched, bodies shiver from the sweating, throats become quenched, dried out by smoking. Baby worms hatch from one end of the cocoon at about three weeks; egg fertilization takes place in the cocoon after the eggs are released from the worm.

"Do you have a cigarette?" Robin asks Jim.

Under normal conditions, red worms stay at home.

"Thanks."

They will not crawl away if adequate food, aeration, and moisture are provided for them. Red worms feed from beneath after they become familiar with their new environment.

INT. FRISK NIGHTCLUB—MIDNIGHT

Shawn and Jim are talking in the hallway. It is very boisterous and loud. Robin keeps signalling Shawn, but it's
unclear exactly what she's signalling. Jim tugs on Shawn's
sleeve.

SHAWN We have a serious problem. Someone hacked into
Robin's computer. I know it isn't you because you're too
mean. But someone knows what's happening, Jimbo. They
tell me they are going to come in and take us down. So
you were right. JIM Wasn't me. One of the girls? SHAWN
Naw. JIM Who? SHAWN Don't know. But they know spe-
cifics. They know stuff even you don't know, that only I
know, that I have on Robin's computer. Hidden stuff—she
doesn't even know about it—maybe it's one of her guy
friends . . . or a brother. JIM So what are we going to do?
Cancel? SHAWN Cancel? You fucking nuts? We're halfway through this. No, we have a thousand dollars worth
of pre-sold tickets, we have another grand coming at the
door, plus whatever else we can manage—you know—in
the back. Let's take the money and run. JIM Right. Sorry,
you're right. I'm kinda wasted. SHAWN No kidding. I'm
sharp. Don't worry 'bout me. Just get the girls to get two
of their friends to get in the coffins; they're being set up
now. We'll have a runner take all the money out the back.

If the cops strike, we take off out the back, right? Get a car for the back. JIM Where's the money now? SHAWN Don't worry about that. The doors open in thirty minutes. Get a car for the back and a runner, even if it's you. JIM Right. SHAWN Everything goes as planned, the deejay, the props, the screaming murder samples, all that stuff. Hell is all around us.

EXT. OUTSIDE FRISK NIGHTCLUB—1:14 A.M.

Jim and Shawn are arguing in front of two trucks when Lee and Steven come out of the back door of the club. Shawn is holding Jim up against a wall. The coffins have been taken off the hooks and loaded carefully into a pickup truck.

JIM Fuck that man, I'm not going anywhere with you, you're a fuckin' psycho. SHAWN Just come with, we'll sort out the split down the road. I'm moving anyway, so, like, you know, my address will be up in the air for a few days. We'll have time to figure something out. Let's just take the money and run. (Jim sees Lee and Steven walking up behind them.) JIM It was supposed to be simple, you and me split the money, we pay the club, the deejay, now what's going on? SHAWN Lee's helping us rob our own venue. Don't you get it!? JIM Think about what you're saying. You're fucked, man. SHAWN I am unknowable, Jim.

You talk shit. You are not iconic. You're a dime store nov-
elty. You're second rate and I hate your fucking guts. You
bring nothing to this equation but a downgraded sense of
crapola. I'm sick of your shit-talking. You talk complete
shit. JIM Shawn, no, please don't do this, just let me go,
just cool off. SHAWN Let you go? Why? You're poison to
my plans. Lee and I are in charge now. You're not going
to mess with my racket. You just swill your wine and take
your pretty candies and think that's life. That's it? It's more
and more. It's detailed. You don't get that. You don't just
fucking show up, you have to work.

The end of the road. The end of the night. Lee is jamming
the third coffin into the back of the pickup truck and sig-
nalling for Steven to get Jim in the back.

SHAWN We're going to split the money up one town over;
we just have to make it look like this place was robbed, you
know, maybe they thought there was something valuable
in the coffins right, like cash or something. JIM There is
something valuable in there! SHAWN The police will deal
with you and your weird fetish. To the park! (Talking to
Jim like he's a child) Jim, give me your wallet. Good boy.
(Lee slaps the money down: three hundred dollars. Looks
at Jim.) LEE Now if you shut up there's more for you, we
just have to get out of here. Now get in the fucking truck.

(Jim turns to Shawn shaking his head.) LEE (nodding to Steven) Do it. (Steven clocks Jim in the side of the head.) LEE Toss him in the back. Shawn you ride shotgun. Steven you ride with the stiffs in the back, keep down. Then we'll go to Crystal's for a nice nightcap. SHAWN No, man, after we sort this out I'm gonna bail. LEE We'll see. You never know what's around the corner, Shawn.

EXT. DRIVING—1:34 A.M.

LEE Left here? SHAWN Yeah. We dump Jim and the caskets here, and rally back to the club. (Reaching for his cellphone) I'll double-check on the girls. LEE They're still in the caskets. Where else would they be, Shawn? SHAWN No they're not, the coffins are supposed to be empty. The girls are supposed to be at the club distracting the deejay we're ripping off, the *club* we're robbing! LEE We took them down off the hooks, three of them. Me and Steven. You saw us. Listen, we're doing it my way. Toss all the crap in the ravine, cut the girls legs up a bit, have them make up a phony story—that they crawled back from the dump spot, escaped Jim, end of story. SHAWN Toss the girls down the hill? ARE YOU INSANE? This is nuts! We'll go to jail. LEE End of story, all right? (Lee clocks Shawn in the jaw; he passes out cold.) LEE (Shouting through the window) Steven, from here on in, you call me Jim or

Shawn. So if the girls run screaming, they know who to name, right? STEVEN Right. (Steven and Lee take Jim and toss him down the hill. His hands and feet are tied.) LEE Why'd you tie him up? Go untie him. Put him at the top of the pile, sorta near one of these babies. (He pats a coffin.) STEVEN Gotta wait till he stops rolling. LEE Looks like he stopped rolling about thirty feet down. Bring him up here, to the lip of the hill, gotta rethink things. I'm taking whats-his-name for a ride. You good getting home? STEVEN Yes. (Down the hill, Jim is barely moving. Steven takes the coffins out one at a time and puts them on the edge of the ravine.) LEE Open this one up first. See who's in what. (Steven opens the first casket. Crystal is inside, blindfolded.) CRYSTAL Robin? Where are you? Shawn? What's going on. (Lee closes the lid.) LEE There's tools in the truck. Can you nail these shut better?

3.

Was she the impetus for all this nocturnal carnage and bashing? Was Shawn that jealous, trite, and cruel? Did he hate Jim that much to treat them all like piñatas?—

In and out of consciousness . . . the world breathes around her. Crystal sees the tears in her stockings come to life, laboratory electrodes, she the willing cadaver watching levers go north and south in grainy ritual. *What did I say? What was the last thing I said?* She passes out in the temporary finesse of the ambulance, face in gauze, life tangled in pre-dawn's fresh take of day.

Robin survives with minor bruising, a sprained ankle. Jim is found a few feet down the hill, visibly shaken, scraped and ready to cooperate. That leaves Kimberly (dead), Steven (found at his parents' home cowering in the garage, sobbing at the steering wheel), Lee, and Shawn.

I am in Crystal's hospital room. She is allowed some visitors. So much to ask. She has a dislocated shoulder.

Poor humerus gone and separated from the scapula at the glenohumeral joint, somehow on the way down that nasty Frisk Park hill. Can't talk about things that will upset her. Stick to the facts, my facts, her facts, the facts they're trying to make functional, like a temporary limb.

Lust dungeon was the tagline or password for the party? That meant you had your ticket on hold and you had to pay the other half. The password varied depending on whether you had one or two tickets on hold, or if you bought all the tickets. You also had a confirmation number. *How much was one ticket for the show on the night of the 29th?* Twenty. *Total?* Yes. Robin and Shawn were obsessed with the party. Jim and I were caught up in it a bit as well, but we had other things to occupy our time. *Like what?* Stuff. *Robin and Shawn talked about it a lot?* It was all they seemed to talk about. Robin had other things she was into as well that she was running off to do, but when we were all together, yeah, they were always cooking up ways of getting more people to come. *What did Robin and Shawn discuss specifically about the party itself?* They were going back and forth. Sometimes Jim would add a suggestion. *What was the atmosphere like?* The weather? *No, the mood during the planning?* Oh, Shawn was shouting and laughing that acoustic hippies aren't doing any sets, no way. *They were arguing?* A bit, yeah. Shawn wanted it to be a big nightclub deal, and Robin wanted her friends to be able to play and draw people to come. Shawn thought it didn't sit well and wasn't the right vibe. He wanted goth cheerleaders and trust fund kids to come.

By late morning Crystal has stumbled from her meds into a more convivial state. She is told that Jim is still meeting with a lawyer and Robin's on crutches, and that Steven is in police custody. She is offered water, bendy straws, straight straws, straws with double joints and ribbed comfort, blue or red. She wants some orange juice, and a brush for her tangled forest of dark brown hair. She has two mugs of cold tea sitting on a radiator within arm's reach of her bed. The nurses keep forgetting to remove them and it's bugging her.

Lacerations to the face, what a way to end a night of dancing. Multiple facial lacerations required plastic surgery, doctors removed crushed devitalized tissue— Crystal's face is swollen; she moves her dainty left hand towards her juice straw . . .

DANCE WITH DEATH MAY HAVE STARTED AS ONLINE PRANK
Sicko coffin club party hoax ends with death of
Maudlin teen writes ███████

A seventeen-year-old girl let out terrifying "murderous
screams" as a coyote attacked her while she was trying
to crawl from a prop coffin. The coffin had been thrown
down the side of a hill as part of a "hoax gone insane"
last night in Maudlin. The coyote left a nine-centimetre
cut on the girl's face. The teen was a part of a terribly
conceived heist, and police still are not completely certain
what motivated the teens to reach the "extreme levels of
violence" that dominated the later part of the evening. "I
felt a pinch at my face, then I sort of passed out," Crystal
Rowles said, noting the coyote left bite holes in her jean
jacket.

A cruel and unbelievably vicious prank perpetrated
upon a group of young girls has pollinated Maudlin City
with the terrible aroma of injustice. A seventeen-year-old
girl is dead at the hands of other teens (a third girl escaped
with a sprained ankle), who allegedly lured her into a prop
coffin at a local club, only to be driven in the back of a
truck and tossed down a hill.

Her parents are shattered and in shock. Her name
was Kimberly Kite, a budding dramatist at the local high
school. "Mom! Mom! Can I go to this party?" Tara Kite

recalls her daughter asking. Her "friends" had contacted Kimberly regularly during the weeks leading up to the party and wanted her to be added as one of the girls in the prop coffins. Tara denied knowing about the coffins being a part of the party. "She loved boating, horseback riding, fishing, cats, hip-hop, and drama, particularly singing. Sometimes," Tara said, "Kimberly could go days in moody irritability, then suddenly perk up." On average, Kimberly was popular in school. "She was loud and boisterous and always singing a song," said a classmate.

On October 27, 200–, Kimberly received a message from two other teens with a new address for the party and instructions "to not tell your mom." Tara recalls that one message from that night simply said: "We can't wait to see you at the party, girl! C U SOON!!!" Investigators say the coffins were designed for theatre, but not safety, and didn't have adequate breathing tubes. However, they know for certain Kimberly's death was the result of impact on the side of a hill, after being tossed from the road, minutes after being taken from Frisk, the club where the prop coffins had been secured by meat hooks and suspended like decorations throughout most of the evening. "It's just so horrifying to think about," one of Kimberly's classmates said. "It's such an awful way to die, to have your last moments be so constricted and— it's just so gruesome."

END OF CLIPPING.

4.

HILLSIDE DEATH PUZZLES INVESTIGATORS. TWO OTHERS
SOUGHT IN KITE'S DEATH. FRISK PARK MURDERERS STILL
AT LARGE. The headlines over the next three days all use
playful, sly language that teeters on the brink of despair
and commerce. LANDSLIDE INVESTIGATION or PROP COF-
FIN SICKOS or DANCE PARTY HOAX WRANGLERS SOUGHT.

Jim stumbles to his feet, gets kicked in the gut a few times
before Lee and Steven drive off with Shawn. Flashlights
appear like migratory June bugs, plucking and bobbing in
the night. A police floodlight shines at the top of the hill
and sirens blare before a coyote bites the side of Crystal's
face. She sees nothing but red and black attack her.

"Down there," gunshot, gunshot, "the coyote has her!"

She wonders what colour she's wearing because all she
sees is black. She sees nothing, she feels gauze. Before the
week is up she's answered the phone a thousand times and

her throat feels permanently parched and full of what feels like viper fang bites. It's all too much . . .

Jim and Steven are held in custody pending further investigation. Questions flood the police stations and school districts. Two others believed to be the ringleaders of the dance hall hoax are sought. Lee and Shawn—what happened to those guys? You get the feeling they just don't want to admit it, come clean and step forward. Whoever is hiding or helping them, please think carefully about the harm you are doing to the Kite family and Kimberly's friends. You have to feel for her friends and family at a time like this.

The skirmish may have started back in the truck just before Steven and Lee decided to take Shawn to Lake Maudlin to toss him in the harbour. They may have taken another route, one more secluded, one where Lee could take his time with Shawn, get his fingernails trimmed, do a few push-ups.

And Lee may have told Steven to go on without him, to take the truck and just, you know, scatter, that he'd find his way back on his own, but for Steven to just lay low for a bit. Steven was picked up shortly after 2 a.m.; Robin and Crystal described the van and those in it within reasonable facsimile. Plus, others knew Steven from the club. There was little else to go on. The mud on the tires led police to a bunch of creeks and off-roads, but they had no luck finding the other two suspects. Steven refused to reveal much to police.

"I'm going to toss you in the fucking lake and throw rocks at you until you're dead, Shawny. What's wrong? Can't talk?" At 3 a.m. Shawn wraps a piece of steel chain around Lee's ankle, pulls him down to the ground. A huge thwack against the rocky ground. Shawn pulls hard on the chain and Lee falls backward, knocking his head. Thwack! Shawn picks Lee up and drags him over to the side of the cliff, about ten feet above the water. Lee wraps his knuckles in the chain, finding it beside his ankle where it had fallen loose. Punch. But Shawn reaches out with his hands, his bony arms. Swings again, missing.

Shawn side-headlocks Lee. In the air now, they connect, squeezing oxygen from one another, and plummet. They pull each other into the water and fall face-first, choking and scratching one another, the steel-linked snake following close behind, sinking, sinking, sinking like a heavy dead ribbon.

The worms that have crowned the inside of my brain—that cerebral kingdom and its moats of grandeur—have withered in the sun. New seasons have kept my mental faculties occupied, elsewhere. Chelsey's another year older, and on a whim we meet up for dinner just to catch up like old friends did in prehistoric times. I use the term prehistoric, if only to make the point that so much has happened, so much history has befallen here, it's hard to see the dirt from the skin. We will only discuss the basics.

I am half an hour early so I busy myself with a coffee a quarter block away and re-read the entertainment section of the newspaper. I can't stand reading the city section anymore, it's like checking my email. No, it's getting better, thankfully, with time. The worms who thorned my brain from the inside, a reverse crown of mischief and battle temptation have withered in the sun and snapped into pieces. New seasons have kept my mental faculties occupied, elsewhere. Chelsey's first question will be, so what have you been doing? Up to? Writing? How's that going?

Did you know Kimberly Kite? No. I saw her once at a party with Robin and some other people. Not really. We were in the same year, I think. I had heard of her only in passing, like, she was at a certain event that a mutual friend was talking about. *Did you know Shawn well?* I thought so. He was hard to read. *Did he ever talk about the coffins?* No, never. He would ask me if I had heard of any good clubs or been to any good parties. We would get pizza, watch movies, make out, have sex. He was kind to me. We were not very serious though. He was intense at times. *Did he ever ask you to do anything?* Yes. I mean, we were together a lot. We spent hours together. *Did he ever tell you to do anything strange, like . . .* S&M? No. No peeing, nothing like that. We slapped each other a couple of times. *Did you know Jim?* Not well. He went to another school, and I heard Robin and Crystal were hanging with him a lot. I only met him like once or twice at one of Robin's parties. *Did Shawn ever say anything negative about Jim?* No, he just stopped talking to him for a while after Crystal. Then he said he was working on the party with Jim and I just figured they'd patched things up. I wasn't with Shawn a lot during that time. I told him she'd do this to him and that they were perfect for each other 'cause they'd both cheat on each other and not care. *After Crystal?* Jim had sex with her while she was with Shawn. *Did you visit Crystal in the hospital?* No. We weren't close. I felt bad for her, and the coyote bite and stuff.

5.

Snow has altered the land; the wisps of new spring have tried to burn things, coming full circle.

Chelsey stands outside the boat restaurant with a twelve-gauge smile. I have been pacing around the parameters for the better part of half an hour, as I'm always early.

Chelsey looks pale and soft. The way I remember her. She's right in front of me like a planet, a page in a book, a familiar cut of a tooth. A soft tooth worn around the neck. I am terrible with fusing these sorts of linguistic declarations; they all turn into pipe bombs.

We have chosen an empty booth in the gutted hull of an old ship, the kind that is on the lake but not really a boat. I'm sure there is some paperwork that certifies its inability to sustain a voyage. I'm so nervous. Maybe some facts about the boat are on the menu.

"If there is one thing you can say about mussels," I say, "it is that they are extremely versatile. But can also be disappointing."

"I liked the ones you cooked for me," Chelsey says. "You're a good cook, Charles."

"Yeah, those *were* good," I go, trying to sound normal, basic.

"Yup."

After a pause I add, "I think a lot depends on the emotional state of the cook and the guests."

Chelsey blinks in what I consider to be agreement.

"Some people put tomato sauce with mussels, but I prefer a simple white wine sauce. They are also delicious marinated, grilled, skewered."

"I'm going to get a salad," Chelsey says, sitting calmly. The candles make her round face and eyes flicker as if a tide were washing over her, as if someone were deliberately trying to make her appear even more beautiful. God will drown with me tonight, I think to myself, and immediately pull back on my negativity reigns. I have this negative stallion I ride on, you see, and some nights I gallop.

"Sometimes, for a bit more flavour, I like adding a pinch or two of saffron for a curry saffron cream."

"You sound like you've been cooking."

They turned it into a restaurant in the late 1960s. It was originally an Adriatic liner, as the menu tells me, "steaming into Maudlin harbour from the former republic of Yugoslavia." I calculate the possibility of being taken out to sea, of sleeping with Chelsey, of accidentally eating one of

Ulysses' cousins. I may be speaking aloud at this point.

"Who is Ulysses?" Chelsey asks. "I mean, not the book right? You're talking about, what, a boat or something, Charles?"

I guess I started rambling about Ulysses when we walked by a fish tank a few moments ago, so no wonder Chelsey asks me about it. So awkward. I don't really explain things properly. This is something I am reminded of when I meet up with Chelsey. This is something I feel right now.

"Ulysses used to follow Cousteau's crew around. It was a big slow fish. The divers would lock him in the anti-shark cage so they could do their work. He was a big slow fish."

Chelsey's eyebrows go up and down; there is a moment where a smile appears but is smudged.

The waitress scuttles up to the table. "How are you this evening?"

"Pleasantly at sea," I say, and it's immediately followed by my brand of awkward apologies.

"Oh right," she says. Chelsey shakes her head in partial disgust.

"Come on," I joke, engaging both women momentarily with my charmless netting, "you must get all sorts of intolerable sea-themed banter here."

"I guess."

This moment is like a thousand other moments: I seem to be insane in the same way over and over, and I'm telling them, two girls, this very fact. Sometimes it's a doctor and a bus driver, or a waitress and an ex-girlfriend. Sometimes they are not even real, just mpegs I've downloaded in string bikinis, bouncing and pulling in front of a computer screen as they hiss and spill their coffee on their robotic laps. And deep down, I know they're totally lying to me but they keep popping up on the screen. Their lies pop up in textual eel bites and my hands type and get bitten and we talk for a decade. Ten minutes. Sorry. I exaggerate sometimes.

Chelsey orders prawn salad and I follow suit, adding, "and can we have an order of the fried calamari?"

Chelsey tells me a dream she had recently where she was in a pink dress in someone's driveway holding a jar of bees.

"That doesn't surprise me," I say.

"Why would you say that?" Chelsey asks. Why is that still written all over her face?

Silence, and it is awkward, but no more awkward than usual. I don't tell Chelsey about the giant wasp that may or may not have been in front of my house a few nights ago. I don't even tell her about robot wasps mimicking wood wasps to save the brains of the future. My brain hurts. It feels like it is in a hurry. The waitress confirms this is a possibility while dropping off some bread and butter in a small red basket.

We used to eat dinner together. I would cook her pork chops. Then one night we went out to eat at a Greek restaurant.

"Remember the lamb chops?"

"Yeah, that was nice."

I begin to worry that we will have nothing to talk about. I am hesitant to order wine, light a candle, or stare at her face.

"I've been with someone for a bit now," Chelscy says, looking straight at me like a television actress. Like a soap commercial. Like a magazine model, looking right at me. She begins to tell me a bit more: how she wanted to tell me about Richard sooner, that it was important for me, especially for a man my age, to confront reality.

Chelsey asks me if I'm seeing anyone. I tell her No. I say the word and I feel its empty cartridge. I want the night to stand still, and end, and break off with us attached to it.

"I like my job, the people are nice," Chelsey says. She has been working with children in a theatre school; she was hired straight from university. She finds the work very rewarding.

"When you wrote about me, it was so nice. No one has ever written about me that way before. But it scared me. Not scared, but it was weird. It was like something that happened to us, that we shared, then it was in a magazine or a journal."

"I just wanted you to feel loved. I wanted you to feel beautiful, and read the way you made me see you, I guess."

"When you wrote about me I felt safe for a while. When we first were together was when I stopped writing in my diary."

"Really?" I have no idea what Chelsey means by this and don't ask for clarification. Salmon swim upstream. I am working on a joke about white flour and salmon in my head when Chelsey shakes her empty glass of water. She has ice cubes in her mouth and comically attempts parlance. We share a smile. That's the only way I've ever imagined how it must be to know me: fun and light and sexy and sleepy, or alert, tense, and anxious. Those are the side effects I encourage. That's how it must be, I think. I tell Chelsey that I'm glad she is happy.

"When we were together," she says, "I thought I wouldn't be good for you."

"Why?"

"You were always taking care of me. Cooking and stuff. Making me laugh. I felt lost."

I don't say anything.

I begin a mental list of foods that have worked on Chelsey in the past: strawberries, truffles, Red Bull, vodka, champagne, and mussels. By worked I mean more associated with, i.e., that we shared.

The calamari comes and Chelsey's eyes light up. She munches on some dangly bits. Her eyes are this big blue afternoon sky edited down to an inch and a quarter. There is an overcast of blinking. The clouds have eyelashes. I'm writing about her on the napkin with my fingertips.

"I guess you go the distance with someone, or I do. I feel like, you know, it was exciting and fresh for so long, and seemed infinite." I finish my speech by saying things get murky, silent, and dark. I tell Chelsey I can't write myself out of love with her or anyone anymore. That eventually I will have to become real.

"But you are real," Chelsey says. She doesn't know what she's talking about. I want to say this to her.

Despite the lure of a variety of seafood entrees, I have returned to the meal we once both ordered: lamb chops. Perhaps the most carnivorous meal a sea person could choose. I eat it slowly, chewing calmly, thoroughly, with inviting, but not suggestive, body language.

Chelsey eats her main course: a small filet of salmon with rice and green beans. I had once cooked a similar meal for her and smile at her. She smiles and flares her tiny nostrils. She sniffs. She snorts. She does cute things and then stops. She says, her tiny mouth overcome with morsels, "I wanna smoke."

I agree that I could have a cigarette, that I could enjoy it right now. We go outside and smoke separate cigarettes. I try to hug her. It's a bit weird. There is no hug; it's avoided, like roadkill or something.

Back inside Chelsey orders a Coke.

"This is the reality I don't wanna face, the reality you've been bragging about, Chelsey," I say with a strange, sweaty grin. I have no idea how my face appears to Chelsey, but she nods, accepting the words.

"There you go, big guy," she says. My sarcasm has been mistaken for enthusiasm. I feel older than ever.

Unlike our time, when we'd sleep beside one another, span stolen hours in her luxurious student bed, we take separate cabs this evening.

"It is essential for the survival of our species," I say, and kiss her forehead before she lowers herself down off the curb into the back seat. I shut the door. Behind me there is a blurry wave of some sort. I have a toothpick in my mouth. The boat gimmick restaurant is stationary in its permanent spot along the dock: a tired whale of a boat, beached in concrete and chain. A real dining freak. I look behind it, out into the black sky and water and feel like the biggest loser.

The waves still come and pull. I can hear everything on earth. There is so much to listen for. There is a future. It will always come. The sand on the nearby beach moves, it is covered in ice. The temperature is dropping. And there comes a time when you have to stop moving sideways and just let it all wash over you. The waves move through and around you. It is what they are supposed to do. You don't always have to remember, I know this now. There is a future, for Chelsey and I, separately. It will always come. The waves still come and pull. Chelsey will visit me in my dreams like a whitecap. She will grow her sexy brown hair and flutter her big, marvellous eyes. She will be a coveted asteroid, a comet I marked with expressive white chalk on the walls of my inner dementia.

I walk farther toward Lake Maudlin, the end of my Chelsey indulgence, my shallow plea. I would give one last great confession, one last symphonic medley, on Maudlin's edge, before returning to bed anew.

The past year, however long these worms have lived inside my brain, these brats, has been a seamless nightmare of vulgar sweat—off-handed, dark, and wrong. I stay another few moments along the beach, now totally chained to my own routine and rust. I remember the fourth-last date with Chelsey, months ago. The steak sandwich I watched her eat. I sulked through her gorgeousness. Her beauty twisted me. Elastics choked the edges of Chelsey's brandied hair, her round face glowed, complementing her bright eyes. But her pretty face had accents of doubt despite wanting me to visit for soup and nursing. She offered me some of her steak sandwich, her French fries; nothing worked and my heart hurt. The more I looked at her beauty, the creepier I finally felt—free and sad. There was a way that I could succeed, but to retrieve these atoms and institute these laws would go against every lifelong self-destructive impulse traditionally catered to.

That time, last winter, after the scent of her steak sandwich left me, and I could still see her red boots down the street, I sprinted to catch her, only to re-live the drudgery of rejection in slow motion—she wasn't bluffing, stalling—*I have to go* . . . and she went . . . and the glint I once saw in her had entered the free-press zone, had turned on its belly and died, carp-like.

That was a while ago. And that was awful.

I coddle the moment and stare into the blank, wet, black lake. I rock and shake in my cold shoes and stare as I always do until the familiar intensity wears off, for now. I say something pathetic to myself, something like, *you can't ignore my passion*—but we always can. We always can ignore passion. Ignore it all. The way things slip too deeply, quick and easy. The way water is infinite, anonymous, and part human.

The buildings have eyes. The lake is asleep.

It is now so very late, and a stereo volume knob is being cranked somewhere by a set of the most sensitive, unprinted hands.

6.

Did you see the coyotes in the news? I had heard of them.
I never thought I'd meet them up close. (Crystal laughs,
continuing) Coyote is the new cosmetic for me, I guess.
Lucky me. I need to rest. Come back later. *Did Jim tell you
that he was going to kill Kim?* No. It wasn't like that. Me,
Robin, and Kimberly all got into the coffins. *When did you
first hear about the coffins?* From Shawn, about two weeks
before. I thought it was a joke. Then I saw them in the
club, hanging from these chains on giant hooks. The truth
doesn't matter. That's what I think. I mean, tomorrow, today, someone is going to get killed. People are more concerned with it, like, you know, it's something they have to
fill out reports about, call people, and get sound bites. The
truth is, it's the last thing on anyone's mind. I mean, I think
that Shawn told Jim some of his plan, but not all of it, and
Lee got word of it and there was a big blow out. (She's tired
and I'm asked to leave the room. I come back four hours

later.) *Sorry to bother you again. Anything else?* I remember hitting the ground and thinking that I was falling. The floor beneath me was gone and I was just plummeting or whatever, just all that dirt suddenly on my tights when I saw that part of the coffin had cracked apart, and dust was everywhere and dirt was in my eyes and nose. It was shocking, and I knew things had gone bad. The top of my casket cracks a bit, right, and I can see the night sky and I'm at the bottom of the hill looking up. Then I remember trying to stand up and falling down on my ass. The next thing Jim is with the police, they are walking toward me, they are pulling Robin from one of the caskets. Then someone says "over there" and points to me. Then they go to Kim's casket and stand around with flashlights, and that's all I remember. Robin and Shawn probably cooked this whole thing up, they were always lying to me about everything, sleeping with each other, other shit. When they were together it was no good. *No one knows where Shawn is?* (She can't handle the question.) *Did you know Lee?* Yes. *How well?* We hung out. *When did you notice the coyote?* I didn't, it just struck me from the right, biting my face until the police shot it.

7.

4:45 PM me: really?

4:45 PM kimberly: yeah

4:46 PM me: wow. that would be great if you could do it . . . i would pay you . . . something

5:07 PM kimberly: oh, to make that movie?

5:09 PM me: 30 seconds, there are tiny cameras in the coffins . . . i was thinking . . . just a girl screaming, blair witch mascara tears, panty scratch

5:11 PM kimberly: I dunno

5:12 PM me: cowgirl hat

5:13 PM kimberly: ahaha . . . well, i will think about it

5:15 PM me: thanks

5: 16 PM kimberly: is there more than one person in it?

5:15 PM me: there are 3 coffins in the club hanging from meat hooks

5:15 PM me: each coffin, one girl or maybe 2. can more than one fit in? this could change! i wish i could talk to you on the phone about it

5:16 PM kimberly: well the thing is i don't know if i have time to do something that complex. i only have 1 coffin, i mean my mom has only one prop coffin

5:17 PM me: crazy, no I was gonna rent them. didn't know your mom had one . . . no no just one

5:18 PM kimberly: and maybe i could just be in it and pretend to sing or something at the party . . .

5:16 PM me: you could spit out glitter or something or ginger ale or champagne

5:20 PM kimberly: oh

5:21 PM me: fake champagne

5:22 PM kimberly: well ok . . . will def think about it

5:24 PM me: I liked kissing you . . .

5:25 PM kimberly: I felt like such an aggressive hungry kisser, I got so embarrassed, and weirded out by my attraction to you, I'm not ovulating . . .

8.

POLICE: "THESE ARE THE FRISK PARK MURDER SUSPECTS"
writes ████

The bodies of two teens known as Lee Showles and
Shawn Michaels have been pulled from Lake Maudlin.
Investigators are satisfied. My manner convinced them.
I offered them some bottled water and shook my head in
astonishment. It was the day after dinner with Chelsey.
I was singularly at ease. They sat, and while I answered
cheerily, they chatted of familiar things, waited for foren-
sics, I guess, dentists, photo labs, digital fingerprints, ac-
countants.

While my hair was still cut straight across my forehead
I walked by the scene where the prop coffins had skied
down so thoughtlessly. Frisk Park. What a name. Just last
week I played at the base of the hill, pulling flowers, re-
membering how Crystal's shoulder had separated, how

she had just popped her head through the crack in the coffin lid when the coyote bit her cheek. Like a baboon or something on a unicycle. Not comical but full of a strength I could never have imagined possible. I mean, happening like that, so drastic, so cruelly potent.

Time passes and it means something else, always has the same cut, like when you look at your teeth or a scar— the same—you can run your tongue along the side and feel how you've deepened the groove a bit in your worry. Your teeth, that is, but your problems probably are no better. No more solved.

For nearly a year, the families who lived along Maudlin City harbour never knew the whole story about the dance party tragedy that occured at the now closed Frisk Park Nightclub. On the night of October 30, 200–, Kimberly Kite's life was cut tragically short when an illegal dance party, alledgedly orchestrated by two teens (one in custody), went tragically awry. And now a third suspect has been tied to the crime as two bodies were just pulled from the icy waters of Lake Maudlin.

I was just walking around my usual route here, where I used to sell water on hot days but, wow, what a sight. Sorry if I'm losing my investigative tone here, but there is nothing much left to investigate. Lee, has been identified as the driver of the van that took the three prop coffins from the club the night in question, some ten months ago, and he tossed them off the side of a small ravine where they hit the bottom of an escarpment area, a micro falls, you could say.

Another teen who survived the dangerous coffin dumping is in psychiatric custody and has not been (at press time) implicated in the death of Kimberly Kite, which is now being dubbed the "Frisk Park Murder."

What happened that night, Robin? I heard shouting, Jim or Shawn, one of them abruptly turned on the other, just before we were tossed down the hill, one of them was begging the other not to do it.

The secret was revealed six weeks later: Robin Beedie, a classmate, invited Kimberly Kite to a "crazy f——— night where we get to be the stars." The same message was sent by another classmate, Jim Helwig, and by Shawn Michaels. Jim has been released pending further investigations.

After their daughter's death, Tara and Rick Kite requested a trust be set up for Kimberly's memory, "something to do with the dramatic arts, something she was passionate about."

END OF CLIPPING.

9.

I just downed 25 mg of Soderiaz. After many weeks of planning, planting, and heavy meditations, I try talking to the garden and the worms in my dead uncle's backyard without having a major anxiety meltdown. (I know if Cate were here, she would suggest the last line should be something to the effect of, "Make him eat 'em, make him eat the little worm.") But I can't focus on the negative, any negative pantomime, including sarcastic discourse, or lessons in disassociation that Cate might suggest. I think eating a worm would be a negative thing.

I can't help it. I am scheduled to love life and the sunshine. I do not hear their tiny millipede phonics anymore. My trademark darkness has dissipated, and my luminous pores are now receiving nutrients and sustenance. Where my throat was sore and dry, where my lips felt shrivelled, where my pupils felt scuffed and raw, where my eye ducts felt gouged by cyclical tears, I can now feel free, real, without psychosis. It's good not to hear anything, for stillness to be gentle and real. No surprises. A cocoon of warmth. Seeding real beauty, bucolic green stems, and lovely puddles. There are no more evil spirits in Maudlin's uniquely cagey garden.

There is only paradise and puddles.

ROBIN
We're mad, bad, and dangerous to know, Crystal!

CRYSTAL
Mwaaw-hahahaah . . .

notes

This project was inspired by two crimes: the New Year's Day 2008 Toronto murder of fourteen-year-old Stefanie Rengel, and the Josh Evans Myspace prank/hoax, particularly well covered in an article in *The New Yorker* by Lauren Collins called "Friend Game" in early 2008.

The voice-over text component in the novel comes directly from *Fictional Dance Party* (Bravo!Fact, 2007) directed by Geoffrey Pugen. I wrote and performed the voice-over for this short video/art project.

The book cover image credit is as follows: Geoffrey Pugen, *Fictional Dance Party*, Untitled 4, 2007, C-print, 20" x 14".

acknowledgements

I would like to thank Halli Villegas for believing in this project, and her tireless staff at Tightrope Books.

Thanks to Jessica Westhead for an early read and story edit, suggestions for lucidity, and for having such great dialogue in her own craft to respond to. Thanks to Tightrope's Shirarose Wilensky for seeing the manuscript into its finality with a careful edit and helpful suggestions, and to Karen Correia Da Silva for the excellent cover design and suggestions. Thanks to Lori for computer hospitality.

Much gratitude also goes to the Ontario Arts Council through the Writers Reserve Program. This program provided me with some collateral during the completion of this book. Parts of *Wrong Bar* appeared in the zines *Hacksaw* (Vancouver) and *Stationary* (Montreal). Some passages appeared in the Hotel issue of *Descant*.

I would also like to thank Jeen, Kerry, Spencer, Jennifer, Nick, Myna, Angela, Mary, Tony, Carey, Conan, Stacey, Kyra, Geoffrey, and Sonja.

trying to get some video off those cameras," said Capt. Street, "and bring a killer to justice." Police are not ruling anything out, but they say there is no indication that this is a hate crime. Police are asking for your help. If you have any information, call them. Pickett, dubbed "The Guy Lombardo of Halloween," died Wednesday night at the West Los Angeles Veterans Hospital. "Monster Mash" hit the *Billboard* chart three times: when it debuted in 1962, reaching No. 1 the week before Halloween; again in August 1970; and for a third time in May 1973. "I want to be like Madonna. I heard she's an Amazon and her muscles are like ropes and her arms are like boa constrictors. You wouldn't want to get caught in a headlock in one of those things. Well actually YOU, you Shawny, probably would, knowing how you are! You are so sweet to say that you like me and all that. You are a gentleman—that's the best way to be. Are you lonely at night? Sometimes when I finish all my work and chatter for the day, there's nothing left but darkness and I can't hide from the loneliness anymore. Luv, Kim." The jingle-like resurrections were appropriate for a song in which Pickett gravely chafed us with the formaldehyde (IUPAC name methanal) chorus: "He did the monster mash . . . It was a graveyard smash." Photo = snuff meets inner dance party extravaganza—too much boob? Maybe. For any of these options, you need to keep the worm's world cool and damp, so covering it is important. Use old ticket stubs—old carpet and canvas are ideal for covering a ground-based worm farm. A seventeen-year-old girl let out terrifying "murderous screams" as a coyote attacked her while she was trying to crawl out of a prop coffin. The coffin had been thrown down the side of a hill